The Bells of Prosper Station

GLORIA PEARSON-VASEY

The Bells of Prosper Station
Copyright © 2022 by Gloria Pearson-Vasey

Fourth printing,
previously copyrighted 2014, 2015, 2019

Also included in "The Hallowmas Train"
published by Tellwell 2021

VICTORIA HALL
PRESS

Tellwell Talent
www.tellwell.ca

ISBN
978-0-2288-8809-3 (Paperback)
978-0-2288-8810-9 (eBook)

by the same author

fiction:
THE SHUSHAN CITADEL
THE DÚNS
THE BELVEDERE AT STONE GATE
ENIGMA CLUB
BLACK SPRINGS ABBEY
THE HALLOWMAS TRAIN

non-fiction:
MEDITATIVE MOMENTS
FRANCISCAN FOOTPRINTS

with J. Kevin Vasey:
THE ROAD TRIP: Life with Autism

TABLE OF CONTENTS

ACKNOWLEDGEMENTS

I was drawn into historical fantasy by a group of high school students in a creative writing class. Their enthusiasm for the fantasy genre set me wondering if our local oil heritage could translate into fantasy. Might the fumes from 19th century oil gushers, fires and nitroglycerine explosions cause some citizens to evolve into timeriders, psychic vampires or guardians?

Thanks to their youthful inspiration, *The Bells of Prosper Station* evolved, blending fantasy with local history, addiction and intervention.

Special thanks go to my readers, Norm Sutherland, Robert and Gini Newman, Liz Welsh, Laurie Vasey, Mary Vasey and Joel Vasey, whose critiquing and suggestions were invaluable.

I also thank the following archivists and librarians who accommodated and assisted my co-op student and me in our research: Lambton Room Research Assistants Pat McEvoy and Colleen McLean; Archivist, Heather Lavallee; Museums Curator and Supervisor, Dana Thorne; Petrolia Library Branch Assistant, Liz Welsh; and Branch Coordinator, Central Region, Kim Frijia.

I am grateful to my Lambton Central Collegiate & Vocational Institute co-op student, Dylan Racher, for motivating me to immerse myself in area history through our many hours of archival research and interactions with historians, archivists, librarians and local businesses.

I sincerely thank members of the Petrolia Heritage Committee and specifically the following local historians: Robert and Gini Newman, who provided photos, articles and detailed information on their beautiful home in Crescent Park; Norm and Phyllis Sutherland who provided a wealth of contacts and anecdotes; John Phair, whose informative publications were a source of inspiration; Liz Welsh for suggestions and reading recommendations; Martin Dillon for his remarkable website; Helen Heisler for providing material and personal tales about the community; Joel Vasey for his research notes and maps; and Joyce Prevett for sharing her amazing postcard collection.

My appreciation is extended to the Petrolia community for spontaneously sharing stories, and exhibiting pride and enthusiasm in the town's heritage and charm.

October 22

One

She felt the rumble of the train before she heard it, a crescendo of approaching power that penetrated her dreams. As the beast neared, the rhythmic beat of wheel pounding rail became audible. She was fully awake now, her every sense alert and filled with dread.

Although on the previous night, the iron monster had thundered through the town without pause, Azur Moonstorey steeled herself for the inevitable signal that it would stop tonight. After all, it was midnight marking the bridge between the twenty-second and twenty-third days in October, twenty-four hours before the train would take on passengers, twenty-four hours until she would board it and be carried off to an alien place to face the enemy.

And then it came, a long haunting whistle followed by two shorter ones. Azur listened as the train approached Prosper Station, bells clanging as it coasted to a brief taunting halt before heading off again into the darkness.

Shivering, she pulled the covers closer, searching vainly for warmth and sleep against the chill settling into her soul. *I'll be ready, damn you*, she whispered. *I will be ready.*

When dawn finally arrived, she donned jeans and sweater, brushed out her long, dark hair and slipped down the narrow back stairs leading to the kitchen. Mavis was already there, puttering about as she prepared coffee, toast and scrambled eggs.

"Morning, honey," said the older woman, giving her granddaughter a searching look. "Looks like you didn't sleep much."

"It stopped at the station last night, Mavis. Did you hear it?"

"No. But I felt it."

"The whistle was so eerie and the bells so…so…"

"Malignant?" offered Mavis.

"Yes, malignant. It's hard to believe you couldn't hear it."

"One of the blessings for aging Sensos is that we can no longer hear that evil sound. But I remember it all too well. Have you decided what to do?"

"You know that I have no choice."

"Oh, but you do," said her grandfather, entering the room and taking his usual place at the table.

"Good morning, Bram." Azur smiled bleakly at the man who had nurtured her since she was four.

"Go back to school before you fail your year."

"I'm not going to fail my year. I'll be back studying in no time."

"University must be more lenient than it used to be," commented the retired professor of ancient languages.

"I've taken a leave of absence. I'll catch up once we have our lives back."

"God help us," sighed Bram. "It would kill me if I lost you too."

"You're not going to lose me," insisted Azur, her words belying her own qualms. "And when I come back with Hilma, you'll have us both again."

"You're as stubborn as your mother was," he said.

"And she wasn't a Senso," noted his granddaughter, attempting levity.

After setting food upon the table, Mavis joined her husband and granddaughter for breakfast.

"Thanks, Mavis," said Azur, pouring coffee for the three of them. She made a pretense of picking at her food despite the knot in her stomach.

"If you're determined to go," said Bram, "your grandmother undoubtedly has vital information to pass on to you."

"I'm counting on that," said Azur.

"She used to ride that cursed train when she was young, and somehow she always managed to return."

"I didn't know that, Mavis! Why didn't you tell me?"

"We didn't want to provide encouragement to you and Hilma, and we were hoping that it would never occur to you to want to ride it."

"In hindsight that was rather naïve," said Bram.

"Why did you do it, Mavis?" her granddaughter asked.

"Young Sensos have always ridden the Hallowmas train as a lark."

"My great-grandparents knew?" asked Azur.

"It wasn't something we discussed with our parents, but they probably guessed."

"What about you, Bram? Did you know?"

"Most town folk have long heard about those reckless young timeriders although few are believers."

"Except, of course, those with personal experience," said Mavis. "All older Sensos."

"I was one of the skeptics until I started courting your grandmother."

"Did you not have a problem returning home?" Azur asked Mavis.

"The saving grace was that we stayed on board."

"You didn't get off the train?"

"The thrill was in the ride itself."

"Perhaps if the girls had been told that much, we'd still have our Hilma," said Bram.

"I don't need your condemnation, Professor Galvinston," said Mavis defensively. "I have enough self-recrimination to pass around many times, thank you. And may I remind you that we jointly made the decision to keep secret our belief that the girls had the sensointuitive trait."

"It seemed right at the time," he admitted.

"Are you saying you never got off the train, that you were never actually in nineteenth-century Prosper Station?" Azur asked her grandmother.

"Oh, I was there once when three of us as teenagers got off on a dare and learned the hard way that there would be no return until All Souls Day. That was the last time I boarded the train."

"If you survived, then so can I," said Azur hopefully.

"It was touch and go for us, but if you insist on going, I'll tell you everything I remember so you're more prepared than we were."

"Of course, Hilma and I *did* know about the train," Azur reminded her grandparents. "Do you remember when we first asked you about it?"

"It was the Hallowe'en when Bleu arrived," said Bram, nodding at the memory. "You girls had been with us for about three years by then."

Prior to that, the children had been living in Indonesia with their geophysicist parents when their mother died of malaria. Distraught, their father brought them back to Canada and entrusted them to the care of their maternal grandparents. Although he intended to reclaim them at a later time, he returned to his study of Indonesian volcanoes and the years slipped away. At first he sent letters and gifts to his daughters but eventually these became rarer and finally stopped.

Azur clearly remembered the Hallowe'en Bram mentioned. She was seven years old and Hilma, five. They had just returned from trick-or-treating, and as they traipsed up the front porch steps, they found the cat sitting at the door. She was a sleek arrogant looking creature with a shiny coat of bluish silver.

"Can we keep it?" Hilma had pleaded.

"Pleeeeeze!" begged Azur.

"It must belong to someone," their grandfather told them. "It's not just an ordinary cat. It looks like a special breed."

"If we can't find its owner, can we keep it?" asked Azur hopefully.

"We'll see," said Bram. "But be prepared for someone to claim it."

"I think it came on the ghost train," said Hilma.

"What are you talking about?" asked Mavis, startled at this first revelation that the girl might possess the genetic mutation.

"You know. The train that whistles in the night. Before the bells ring at the station."

"We've had no trains in Providence Crossing for years," Bram told the child emphatically. "There are no rails for a train to ride on and the station is now a library."

"I heard it too," said Azur.

"You heard the *wind*," insisted Mavis, turning to her older granddaughter.

"No more nonsense about a ghost train," said Bram firmly.

The little girls regarded their grandparents questioningly, reading in their faces a gravity that demanded the topic be dropped.

In the end, no one came for the cat. It adopted the family on Crescent Park as its own and they called it Bleu, spelling it the French way because of the cat's aristocratic appearance and mysterious manners.

From that time on, the girls heard the train whistles and bells every late October. On those special nights, they slept together in Azur's bed so that they could whisper and giggle in delicious excitement. They were aware that their grandparents were especially vigilant on those autumn nights, careful that no one ventured outdoors through door or window, which added to the thrill.

Two

Dillian Witherton, red hair tied back in an unruly knot, jogged around the tree-lined hub of Crescent Park. Approaching the Galvinston home, she observed a solitary figure sitting pensively on the wide verandah, feet propped on a wicker ottoman.

"Azur?" she queried as she hurried up the walkway of the impressive Italianate structure.

"Dilly!" exclaimed Azur, jumping up and running to meet her friend. "What are you doing here?"

"Checking up on you," said Dilly.

"You came home because of me?"

"I thought you could use some support."

"I'm stunned! When did you arrive?" asked Azur.

"Last night. I told Mom I had permission to do an off-campus project."

"What project would that be?"

"Composing autumn scenes in various media."

"Sounds interesting."

"That's not why I'm here, Az, you goose. I'm going with you and don't give me a hard time."

"I can't let you. Neither of us has any idea about what we might encounter."

"What if I were to tell you that I have my own reasons for going?"

"Yeah?"

"Yeah! My great-great-grandfather was implicated in the murder of a woman in a hotel. My family has always considered him innocent."

"This happened in Prosper Station?"

"Yes."

"You lie!"

"No, it's true."

"Was he found guilty?" asked Azur, caught up in the whodunit.

"He died at the scene, shot dead by a lodger at the same hotel," said Dilly.

"Let me guess. While I'm finding my sister, you'll be solving your family mystery."

"Sure. Why not?"

"Did you hear the train last night?" asked Azur.

"How could I not? It was terrifying," said Dillian. "All the more reason you need me. Hey! Why the tears?"

"I can't believe you'd do this for me."

"Well look who's here. Another truant," said Bram, walking around from the back of the house, rake in hand.

"Hello there, Mr. Galvinston," said Dillian. "We truants stick together."

"Still enjoying Fine Arts?" he asked, wondering if she had dropped out of school.

"So much that it hardly seems like study!" she exclaimed. Dillian's acute sensory system gave her an appreciation of colour, scent and texture that allowed her to totally immerse herself in painting, sculpture and art of every type.

"You're not sick, are you?" asked Bram.

"No, I'm fine."

"Are you here to dissuade Azur from taking that cursed train?"

"I'm going with her, Mr. Galvinston."

"Dillian," said Bram, "I don't think either of you should be doing this. It's extremely risky. Does your mother know?"

"Mom doesn't believe in all this senso-stuff, which is just as well." Dillian had acquired her genetic trait from her father's side of the family. When her unusual abilities manifested themselves shortly after her parents' divorce, the child soon learned that her mother considered it childish make-believe. She considered herself a lonely anomaly until she shared her secret with the Moonstorey sisters, cementing their trust and friendship forever.

"What does she think happened to Hilma?" asked Bram.

"She doesn't know, but it frightens her and she's always warning me to be wary of pretty much everything."

"Let's go into the house and find Mavis," Azur said to her friend. "She used to ride the train when she was young and once she actually got stranded in Prosper Station for a few days. Can you believe?"

"You never told me that!"

"I just found out myself. Mavis can help us prepare – that is, if you haven't changed your mind."

"My decision is firm!"

The young women found Mavis in her study poring over an old journal. Without looking up, she said, "I'm reading the diary notations I made upon returning from my train adventure, honey."

"We have company," Azur told her grandmother.

"Good heavens, Dillian!" exclaimed Mavis. "What are you doing here?"

"I'm going to ride the rails with your granddaughter."

"Are you sure you want to do this?"

"I'm here aren't I?"

"Does your mother know what you're doing? Does Graeme?"

"Graeme thinks I'm doing a two-week off-campus art project somewhere – I left him a deliberately vague message."

"And your Mom?"

"She noticed that Azur was home and will expect me to hang out with her."

"Dillian, I confess it would reassure me to have you accompany Azur, but at the same time, I'd feel tremendous guilt allowing you to be exposed to such danger."

"You're not *allowing* me, Mrs. Galvinston. I'm an adult and I have free will."

"I'm uncomfortable about you deceiving your mother and your fiancé."

"It would be impossible to explain it to either of them. They're both in denial about supernatural stuff," said Dillian. "But I feel an urgency to be at Azur's side to confront whatever has taken Hilma."

"Sensointuitives *are* warriors," noted Mavis, studying her granddaughter's friend thoughtfully.

"*I* don't feel like the warrior type," confessed Azur. "I think I'm rather cowardly."

"You're cautious, dear, not cowardly," said Mavis. "There's a big difference. Warriors do feel fear."

"Hilma was fearless."

"Your sister was impulsive," said Mavis. "Caution makes for a better warrior."

"Do you have some words of wisdom for us, Mrs. Galvinston?" asked Dillian.

The older woman studied them thoughtfully. "Sit down, girls," she said. "There are several things you need to understand about yourselves and your town."

She began by reminding them that Prosper Station received its name because of the prosperity brought to the community by the discovery of oil in the 1850s. Geologists were attracted to the area by the tar-soaked gum beds. The first oil well was dug in the county in 1858, producing crude oil which at the time was used for illuminating oil for lamps. The rush was on and by 1861 four hundred wells had been dug.

"A history lesson is important to our safety?" queried Azur mischievously, emboldened by her friend's presence.

"Don't be impertinent, young lady. I'm getting to the critical part. Prosper Station hit its first gusher in 1866 producing two-hundred-and-sixty-five barrels a day. It was incorporated as a village that very year, attracting oil men from far and wide. More than forty years of prosperity followed. At one point, the town had the highest per capita income in Canada."

"Prosperity, Prosper Station," said Dilly.

"Exactly. Now pay attention, ladies! During this time, the town became steeped in oil and its by-products. Because of the technology available in those early days, there were frequent fires, nitroglycerine explosions and gas vapours everywhere. Do you see where this is leading?"

Azur and Dilly looked at her quizzically.

"Dear Lord, girls! Think environmental consequences."

"This has something to do with the train?" asked Azur.

"Very much so. You see, the explosions, fires and vapours led to mutations," explained Mavis.

"Resulting in Sensointuitives!" exclaimed Dilly.

"I'm a mutant?" asked Azur.

Her grandmother nodded. "A very specialized one. Sensointuitives are gifted with acute sensory aptitudes as well as highly developed intuitive abilities."

"This is good, right?" wondered Dilly.

"It's wonderful when you use your abilities wisely," Mavis assured her before continuing. "Now when you leave modern Providence Crossing and arrive in Prosper Station, you will meet other mutants."

"Oh, no!" said Dilly and Azur in unison."

"You will meet a few sensointuitive humans like yourselves, and you'll also encounter shape shifters called Novapetrols and

Faefumes. Novapetrols will assist you, but Faefumes are psychic vampires."

"There are shape shifters there?" wondered Azur.

"And vampires?" asked her friend.

"*Psychic* vampires," repeated Mavis. "They emit seductive fumes while absorbing their victims' vitality and energy. One of these most likely has Hilma."

"Can you escape from them, or is it hopeless?" asked Dilly, shuddering.

"Escape is possible, but victims feel profound tranquility or euphoria. It's like taking drugs. Once they've experienced it, they're drawn to return again and again."

"And the other kind, the Nova…" wondered Azur.

"Novapetrols. You'll recognize them by their blue colouration. They provide protection to time travellers and you must seek one as your guardian as soon as you arrive – if one doesn't approach you first."

"Why would they approach?" asked Dilly.

"Novapetrols seem to come when they sense a timerider is in danger."

"You said there were sensointuitive humans there," said Azur.

"That's right. You'll find them in nineteenth century Prosper Station, back in its Victorian heyday. People will be going about their business as in the early 1890s, dressed in Victorian clothing, walking on plank sidewalks and riding bicycles on dirt streets. You'll see horses and carriages, oil barons, laborers and servants. Most of these people will not be able to see you."

"We'll be invisible?" asked Dilly.

"Except to the mutants," nodded Mavis.

"Which includes sensointuitive people," said Azur.

"Yes. I was getting to them. Although sensointuitive capabilities were already evolving in Prosper Station in the late nineteenth-century, people possessing the mutation were guarded about revealing this for fear of being labeled witches. However, they've come to see timeriders as kindred souls and tend to assist them whenever possible."

"How will we recognize them?" asked Azur.

"They'll be the people looking *at* you rather than *through* you."

"Is that where we'll find Hilma?"

"Sadly, I doubt it. No, she'll most likely be in the dark dimension named Vapourlea by the shape shifters who dwell there."

So Prosper has three dimensions?" asked Dilly.

"Correct. Modern Providence Crossing, nineteenth-century Prosper Station and Vapourlea."

"How will we get to Vapourlea?" asked Azur.

"That I don't know. The three of us who disembarked when we were young managed to resist the seductions of the Faefumes because a Novapetrol encouraged us to avoid Vapourlea until the Hallowmas train could pick us up at the stroke of midnight between All Hallows Eve and All Saints Day."

"Are you saying that we'll have to let the Faefumes admit us to Vapourlea?"

"I'm afraid so."

"My head is spinning," said Dilly. "What else do we need to know?"

"Trust your senses and intuitions. And seek out a blue guardian."

"How should we dress and pack for our trip," asked Azur.

"Pack whatever clothing you can fit in a medium-sized duffle bag. You'll need stretch pants or leggings, long-sleeved blouses, vests, stoles for warmth, basic underclothes. Bring a waist bag in lieu of a purse. I'll make you both some long slitted skirts to wear over the leggings."

"Why would we be wearing leggings under long skirts?" asked Azur.

"So your legs aren't exposed if you have to run. The ability to run is also why the skirts will have slits."

"We'll be worrying about our legs while trying to escape some crazed shape shifter?"

"Yes, granddaughter. Think Victorian decorum."

"What should we do about food?" asked Dillian.

"What should we do about money?" asked Azur.

"You won't require either," said Mavis.

Three

"Azur will be right down," Bram told the young man standing in the hallway admiring the magnificent winding staircase leading to the upper floor.

"How long have you lived in Providence Crossing, Dr. Barkley?"

"Just since summer, Mr. Galvinston. Please call me XT."

"XT?"

"Xavier Tennyson," the man smiled. He looked up at the sound of brisk footsteps running down the stairs.

"Here's my granddaughter, now," said Bram. "She's also in the medical field," he added proudly.

"Delighted to meet you, Miss Moonstorey," said the man, warmly shaking Azur's hand. "What area of medicine are you in?"

"I'm a Registered Nurse studying to become a Nurse Practitioner."

"An increasingly popular field," he noted.

"And badly needed," Azur retorted.

"I was implying that," said XT.

Azur had little time for casual chitchat with a stranger, even an attractive one like this young physician. "Let's go into the parlour," she said peremptorily, leading the way into a cozy sun-splashed room decorated in tasteful antiques. They sat opposite each other, Azur on a floral settee and XT on a blue upholstered Louis XV armchair.

"Thanks for making time for me," said XT.

"My grandmother tells me you're a neurologist, Dr. Barkley."

"XT."

"Pardon?"

"My name is Xavier Tennyson, but the name is strictly for certificates. I've always been XT."

Azur nodded and smiled absently. She wished that today of all days, her grandmother had not agreed to a visitor.

"And you've set up practice here?"

"Yes in neurology. I'm also doing on-call days in the Emergency department two days a week."

"The other doctors appreciate that, I'm sure."

"I believe so, plus working in the ER increases my contact with the community."

"What made you decide to come to Providence Crossing?"

"My family used to visit my aunt here when I was a child, and I've always liked the place. But the reason I moved here is because I wanted a quiet place to carry out my research."

"What are you researching?"

"Emanations and other exceptional sensory abilities."

"Providence Crossing is certainly the place to come for that," said Azur wryly. "I guess you've heard of my grandmother's special gifts."

"I understand you have them too, Miss Moonstorey."

"I'm rather ordinary, actually."

"There's nothing ordinary about you," said XT with an intensity that made her blush.

A soft knock upon the door announced the arrival of Mavis carrying a tray with tea and buttered scones.

"We don't have a lot of time today" said Mavis as she distributed refreshments. "Nonetheless, I was looking forward to meeting a relative of Janet Tennyson. Janet was a dear friend of mine."

"Thank you," replied XT. "I've been told that you and Aunt Janet used to work together and that you were both very gifted."

"Yes. Janet was a pharmacist during the time I was working as a midwife. Were you also told about our reputations?"

Now it was XT's turn to redden. Azur watched the exchange with amusement.

"I'm more interested in fact than rumour, Mrs. Galvinston," said the young doctor earnestly.

"I'm teasing you," said Mavis kindly. "I know that some people called us witches but these same people came to us for help when they had health concerns."

"In my research on sensory and intuitive abilities, I've come across the term, sensointuitive. It seems to result from a genetic trait present in some families, including my own. Furthermore, it seems to be more prevalent in this area."

"Because of the nitroglycerine explosions, fires and gaseous vapours," said Azur, sharing her newly acquired knowledge.

"Oh, when the oil was discovered here in the nineteenth century," said XT attentively. "Toxicity in the environment?"

"That's right," said Mavis. "Apparently it caused genetic mutations. Have you come across that in your research?"

"No," said XT. "But it's the kind of important detail I'm hoping to discover in this town. Would the two of you be willing to participate in a study?"

"We're very busy right now," said Azur with growing impatience. "Perhaps we can discuss this another time."

"Sorry," said the young man. "I should have realized this was not a good time for you."

"We really will have you back another time," Mavis assured him.

"I wish you success in finding your sister, Miss Moonstorey."

"Are you a Sensointuitive, XT?" asked Mavis. This young man seemed to know a lot about them for a newcomer.

"I wish I were," said the man. "I have a genuine interest in these matters because of my family genetics and because I have an autistic brother who sees auras around people. The auras come in a variety of colours providing sensory and intuitive information. It's piqued my curiosity about possible commonalities between autistic and sensointuitive abilities."

"Interesting," commented Mavis.

"I know you're under a lot of stress right now but before I leave, can you clarify the significance of this time of year?"

"What is it you wish to know?" asked Azur, standing.

"Why did you leave your studies to come home a few days ago, the same time of year that your sister disappeared?" he asked Azur.

"Are you a stalker, Dr. Barkley?"

"Forgive my persistence but I know about the Hallowmas train and I believe that this is a critical period for my research."

"If you already know all these things, why are you asking questions?" asked Azur.

"*I'm* wondering why you called it the Hallowmas train," interjected Mavis.

"I thought that's what it was called," said XT, slightly flustered. "It was my understanding that, after delivering passengers to Prosper Station, the train returns to modern Providence Crossing during Hallowmas."

"Hallowmas being All Hallows Eve, All Saints' Day and All Souls' Day," contributed Mavis.

"Is it true, Mavis?" asked Azur. "Does the train only return at that time?"

"Yes," she said. "Returning timeriders must board the train at midnight between All Hallows Eve and All Saints' Day in order to reach Providence Crossing on November 2, All Souls' Day. Otherwise, they must remain until the following year."

"Is that what happened to Hilma?" the young man dared to ask.

"I think we've answered all your questions for now, Dr. Barkley," said Azur dismissively.

"I know I'm coming across as rather abrupt and insensitive," said XT apologetically. "But time is short and I've been waiting for you to come home so that I could speak with you."

"This is not a good time," said Azur.

"I wanted to contact you earlier," he said.

"We'll talk another time."

"Is there any possibility of you including me in your imminent plans?" he persisted desperately. "I'd be so honoured."

"Really, Dr. Barkley, your tenacity is quite annoying. I must say good-bye now."

XT Barkley reluctantly moved towards the foyer. "Do people who lack your giftedness ever board the train?" he asked as he was ushered out through the door.

"Only Sensointuitives can ride the train, XT," said Mavis. "Other mortals can neither see nor sense its presence in any way. Consider yourself fortunate."

DAY 2

October 23

Four

The train rumbled through the night, calling out seductively to Sensointuitives as it drew ever closer to the slumbering town of Providence Crossing.

While still in the distance, Steam Engine 330 sent several short blasts into the crisp October night, warning anything in its path to clear the tracks. Soon thereafter, it announced its approach to the station in standard railway code, two long, haunting whistles followed by a final short one.

The ghostly sound sent shivers down the spines of the handful of people waiting on the station platform.

An hour earlier, Azur Moonstorey had been lost in dreamless sleep mercifully induced by her vigilant grandmother's herbal tea. Sleeping in an adjacent upstairs bedroom, her friend, Dillian Witherton, was similarly somnolent due to the aromatic brew.

The women's duffle bags had been carefully packed and their clothing laid out in readiness for a journey to the past. Stretch pants, layered tops, waist bags, walking boots. Mavis had worked into the late evening creating flowing skirts with side slits that extended almost to the waist bands.

"They'll look like regular Victorian ladies at first glance — but they won't be hampered by restrictive clothing," Mavis told Bram.

At half-past-eleven, she gently shook the pair awake. "It's time," she told them.

"Did I actually sleep?" asked Azur in disbelief.

"Soundly," said Mavis.

Ten minutes later, the young women were in the Galvinston front hall exchanging lingering hugs with Bram and Mavis. Then baggage in hand, they set out into the autumn night. The clip clop of their leather boots seemed exceptionally loud in the eerie silence preceding midnight. No brittle fall leaf rustled in the breezeless night. No dog barked from back yard or alley.

Walking briskly away from the gothic homes of Crescent Park, they soon reached Main Street where they turned left toward their destination, Providence Crossing Public Library.

Formerly the Grand Trunk Railway Station, the library was constructed of red pressed brick and white stone in the eclectic Queen Anne Style typical of early railway architecture. On each end, capped with bellcast roofs and graceful supporting brackets, were circular turret rooms which served as separate waiting areas for men and women in an earlier era. A square tower with fan transom dramatized the front entrance.

Azur and Dilly stood at the base of the library's wide cement steps gazing uneasily at the entryway. No light shone through the thick leaded glass above the wide front doors or from any of the building's windows. For a fleeting moment, Azur considered turning back.

"Do you think there's anyone inside?" whispered Dilly.

"Guess we should find out," said Azur.

Tentatively, they climbed the steps. Although both doors had thumb latches, the door on the left was fixed in place. Azur tentatively approached the right door, the one designed to open, pressed the latch and pushed. The door opened easily, admitting Azur and Dilly to a library bright with lights.

"Strange that we couldn't see lights from outside," whispered Dilly.

There was no librarian in sight but three men sat at reading tables, bent studiously over the books that lay open before them. Two of the men sported navy blue jackets and the third wore a grey windbreaker, collar pulled up at the neck. The women seated themselves at empty computer carrels in the north section from where they regularly glanced at the library clock ticking away the minutes.

When the clock hands reached twelve o'clock, all lights suddenly dimmed to the softer glow of gas lamps. Pastel interior paint faded away to reveal walls of richly paneled Georgian pine. Bookshelves and library furniture disappeared, replaced by wooden benches dispersed around a central waiting room. A baggage room materialized at the station's east end and a ticket office near the back door.

"Your tickets, young ladies," called a uniformed man at the ticket window. Azur and Dilly rose from the bench on which they now found themselves sitting.

"Hope Mavis was right about not needing money," whispered Azur to her friend.

"Tickets are pre-paid, ladies," said the agent jovially, holding out double tickets which each gratefully accepted.

"Remember to tuck away the return portion in a safe place," he advised. "That is, if you plan to return." He chuckled at his own humour.

A second man, also in natty railway uniform, stepped up to the women and moved their bags closer to the rear door. It occurred to Azur that the railway agents were the two readers in navy blue jackets. She looked around for the third man, the one in the grey jacket, and there he was, smiling sheepishly.

"Dr. Barkley!" she exclaimed. "What are you doing here?"

"I walked through the front door about five minutes before you did," he said. "It was easier than I expected."

Azur worried that his arrival would complicate their plans.

Cheerfully extending his hand to Dilly, Xavier Tennyson introduced himself. "I'm XT Barkley," he said.

"Pleased to meet you. I'm Dillian Witherton."

Azur chewed her lower lip in exasperation.

"Better get your ticket," Dilly said to the man, eying him curiously. As XT Barkley walked toward the ticket booth, she asked her friend, "How do you know him?"

"We just met. I'll tell you later."

XT accepted his tickets from the agent, seemingly unperturbed that the man glowered at him wordlessly. He handed his bag to the baggage handler and joined the women.

"Ladies, gentleman, follow me, please!" announced the baggage man, exiting through the back door and placing the bags on a wheeled cart.

Azur, Dilly and XT followed him along a lengthy wooden platform stretching north behind the station. The agent moved the luggage from cart to platform a few feet from the steel railway tracks while the trio stood anxiously facing rails which had begun to hum and tremble.

Moments later, they turned their heads toward a rumbling sound coming from afar. Off in the distance, insistent blasts and long, eerie whistles caused the passengers to shiver and huddle more closely together. The rumbling crescendoed into a roar as Steam Engine 330 rushed toward the depot.

Anxiously, they peered northward into the blackness until they saw a pinpoint of light.

"Here it comes," said Dilly.

The light grew larger and brighter before the train proclaimed its imminent arrival in long and short whistles. Then, with bells clanging, the black iron monster pulled noisily into the depot.

Scarcely had the train come to a full stop when steps were lowered from car to platform. A man smartly attired in navy blue vest, jacket and pants complimented with white shirt and black pill box hat appeared in the doorway of the coach. Polished brass buttons adorned vest and jacket while above the hat's shiny leather bill were grey braid and a brass plate etched with the word, CONDUCTOR.

"All aboard," shouted the conductor, snatching bags from the baggage man and tossing them up into the coach car.

"Watch your step," he instructed Azur in a pleasant manner, taking her by the elbow to assist her up the steps.

Upon entering the coach, Azur noted rows of empty leather seats elegantly covered with lacy back cloths. She was about to take a seat near the front when she felt the train lurch forward, steam hissing and engine growling. Startled, she looked towards the entrance. The door was already closed and the steps retracted.

She tried to run to the door but was pushed firmly into her seat by the conductor.

"Let me out!" she screamed.

"Now, now," he said calmly. "You don't want to stumble and hurt yourself."

Azur moved to the window to see Dillian Witherton and Xavier Tennyson Barkley running along the platform beside the departing train. When the iron beast picked up speed, she caught a final glance of her wildly waving companions, looks of horror upon their faces.

"Look what you've done!" she wailed, but her words were swallowed by the hiss of steam, the clanging bells and the rumbling of the train leaving Prosper Station.

"It seems your friends didn't want to catch this train," said the conductor. "Pity. Their baggage is already on board."

"Liar!" she yelled, enraged and frightened.

"How unladylike," observed the man primly. "Perhaps they'll come another night.

"Is that even possible?" she asked tearfully, realizing that further outbursts, as well as being futile, might prove detrimental.

"Oh, yes. We'll be taking on passengers for a few more days."

Five

"Sit back and enjoy the ride," said the conductor to his sole passenger.

Fighting panic, Azur made an effort to comply. She peered through the window as the train picked up speed and, against the outer blackness, could see only her reflection in the glass. The reflection faded when the train entered a tunnel. Rough stone walls flashed past, illuminated dimly in the light of the coach's oil lamps before blurring into fluidic streaks when the iron beast seemed to leave the tracks. Pushed back into her seat by the gravitational force of the beast's flight, Azur grasped the carriage arms and closed her eyes until she could again feel tracks beneath the speeding coach.

"Your tea, Mademoiselle," said the conductor placing a serviette upon her lap and setting out refreshments on a portable linen-covered table.

Absently, Azur sipped tea from a gold-rimmed china cup bearing the railway logo and selected a dainty sandwich from a matching china plate. Once she began to nibble, she realized that she was unaccountably famished. Soon every sandwich and mini cake was gone. Silently, the conductor removed the salver.

Lulled by the clacking rails and the gently swaying cars, she nodded off.

"Prosper Station!" called the conductor.

Azur awoke with a start to hear clanging engine bells announcing arrival. Somewhat dazed, she allowed herself to be escorted from the train and onto a wooden walkway running north-south along the tracks. The walkway, dimly lit by a single gas lamp, was perpendicular to a raised platform reached by six wide steps.

She looked around in confusion for a familiar landmark.

"Where's the station?" she asked.

"Straight ahead," said a porter picking up her bag and bobbing his head in the direction of the raised platform.

It was then Azur noticed an unpretentious two-storied wooden structure, its lower windows illuminated by flickering oil lamps, the upper windows black. A long low shed was attached to the north side of the building and on the south side was a squat building that might have been for coal or wood. Or an outhouse?

This building clearly lacked the elegance and amenities of the one from which she had recently departed.

"It doesn't look like the Station and it's facing the wrong way," she said.

"Looks alright to me," said the porter setting her bag near the bottom step.

"But the station should be brick and closer to Main Street," she protested. "It should be where that big wooden building is."

"That's Huchson's lumber and coal, Miss."

"It's all wrong."

The porter shrugged and bent to retrieve the unclaimed luggage belonging to XT and Dilly. "I'm taking your friends' bags inside so they can find them when they arrive," he commented.

"My friends are coming?" she asked hopefully.

"I suppose," he said. "Why else would they send their luggage ahead?"

Her short-lived relief quashed, Azur looked about uncertainly as the porter ascended the stairs.

"How did you know the luggage belonged to my friends?"

The porter ignored her question. By now he had reached the station entrance and stood with his hand on the door knob. "Is someone coming to meet you, Miss?" he asked.

"No," she replied in a small voice.

"It's late for a young woman to be out alone. You'd better go directly to your lodgings 'cause we're closing now."

"I have no lodgings," she said weakly. But the porter was already inside and she heard the bolt click in place as the station door was locked.

"What happened to the red brick station?" she asked a man who was loading supplies from the railway platform onto a wagon. "Excuse me, sir," she repeated more loudly.

The man was either deaf or deliberately ignoring her, she thought, until he looked through her to speak to a boy standing nearby.

I'm invisible to them! she realized in alarm.

Azur looked around for the conductor, only to discover that the train was nowhere in sight. How had she missed the clamour of bells and the hissing steam blasts preceding departure? How had she heard no wailing farewell whistle while the train disappeared into the distance?

In no time at all, the men on the loading platform finished their work. Lights within the depot were extinguished and doors bolted. A light flickered briefly upstairs, presumably the station master making his way to bed.

Azur watched helplessly as the workers slipped away to their homes leaving her totally alone outside the deserted station.

The flickering glow of oil fueled street lamps cast small circles of luminosity along the business section of Main Street. All else was darkness. Raising her face skyward, Azur noticed the widened crescent of the waxing moon. She recalled Mavis telling her that this moon phase was a time for friendship, courage and success. Why then did she feel devoid of all three attributes?

Suddenly, Azur felt something unseen brush against her as a seductive voice quietly intoned, "Lovely lady, how kind of you to visit."

She froze in fear, holding her breath. Then cool fingers caressed her face. She gasped.

"Who's there?" she whispered.

The silence that engulfed her was more terrifying than the mystery voice or the chilly touch.

"Help me, somebody help me," she whimpered.

"I'm here," said an agreeable male voice.

A tall being with dark almond-shaped eyes stood before her. Attired in soft leather leggings and tunic, he had blue skin and shoulder-length black hair.

Azur regarded him wordlessly.

"I am Zhiab," he said.

"Was it you who touched me?" she asked.

"No," he assured her. "I am a guardian."

"A guardian?"

"Yes, a Novapetrol."

"Oh, thank heavens," she said. "My grandmother told me to look for you if you didn't approach me first."

"You must take shelter until the dawn," said Zhiab.

"Where?"

"Several guesthouses are nearby."

"Will you take me to one?"

"You must do this yourself," he said kindly.

"You're not leaving!" she cried.

Zhiab nodded slightly. "I will come when you are in peril."

"I'm in peril now!"

"Only if you don't take cover."

"I don't know my way around!"

"Turn on your aptitudes, young Senso," he said while fading from sight.

"Zhiab, where are you?"

Azur sensed that she was now truly alone. Shivering and clutching her belongings, she took a few timid steps to better look around. East of the depot, a two-storied brick building backed by wooden freight sheds was somewhat recognizable as the VanTuyl and Fairbank Hardware of modern Providence Crossing. Familiarity ended there. From where she stood, nothing else looked remotely similar to the town she called home.

Opposite the railway yard on the south side of the street was a large building, 'ANDERSON HOUSE' printed across its wooden front. A light shone faintly in a third floor window. Probably the owner or a maid, she thought.

West of the station was a smaller wood-framed hotel with rolled-up awnings above the windows of its lower floor. At back of the hotel stood a brick building with a sign reading 'FLETCHER HOUSE LIVERY & STABLES.' The latter was in darkness but the hotel itself had lights in one downstairs window and two upper ones.

Azur commanded her unwilling feet to move toward the closer hotel, Fletcher House. In the nighttime stillness, the sound of her boots seemed alarmingly loud. She stepped from the boardwalk onto the dirt road separating depot from hotel. It was a relief to her senses to walk upon the quieter earth, but all too soon, she was on the hotel's wooden walk, clopping along.

"Why would I want to turn on my aptitudes, Zhiab, when I'm trembling with what I'm already capable of feeling?" she muttered.

Because you are on a dangerous quest. It's imperative that you learn to liberate your powers.

"Zhiab?" she asked, looking around expectantly.

Receiving no further response, Azur perceived that she was again alone. Fearfully, she hurried around to the front of the hotel and frantically pulled on the heavy door. It opened with surprising ease into a darkened lobby with a reception desk, a staircase leading upward and two doorways providing access to other ground floor areas. The desk was unattended, but light came through a doorway on the left.

Azur followed the light into a long, narrow saloon, its well-stocked bar occupying one side of the room's length. Towards the back of the dim room, a solitary patron leaned over his drink, one foot supported on a brass railing. Reflected against a large, elaborately framed mirror, a bar tender polished glasses. Behind him, a young woman wearily mopped the floor.

Azur approached the bar keeper. "Excuse me, Sir," she said. "I need a room and there's no one at the desk."

"Closing time," said the keeper to the drinker, unaware of the young timerider standing nearby.

"You said tha' already," replied the man at the bar, speech slurred.

"The Women's Christian Temperance ladies will revoke my licence."

"Wouldn't want those wild women all over you now, would ya." The man guffawed at the image conjured up in his inebriated mind.

"I have to get up in another few hours," complained the server. "And so does Miriam." He bobbed his head in the direction of the girl mopping.

"Okay, okay," said the man, leaving the bar and stumbling toward the lobby. Azur watched him ascend the stairs. She waited until he reached the top before following him to the upper storey.

Six

Although she tried to walk lightly upon each step, several of them creaked loudly as she climbed upward. At one point, the man from the saloon turned around to see who was behind him. The timerider froze. Satisfied that he was alone, the man continued climbing.

Azur reached the top in time to see the man enter a door at the far end of a narrow hall. A single lighted wall sconce enabled her to see several doors on either side. The first door she tested opened to noisy snores from within. The next couple of doors were locked. Then there was a small room containing an elaborate claw-footed bathing tub and an enameled sink.

Finally she entered an unoccupied room facing the front of the hotel. She shut the door behind her and leaned against it in relief. The room contained a mirrored chest of drawers, a wash stand, a wooden chair and a bed. There were wooden clothes pegs on one wall, a kerosene lamp and candles on the chest of drawers, a china wash basin with matching ewer on the stand. Faint light entered the room from a street lamp on the walkway below.

Azur set down her bag and hung her shawl on a peg. She opened the window to let in fresh air and stuck her head out to get a wider view of the street. Across the way, the lamp in the third floor window of Anderson House had been extinguished and, with the exception of faint pools of light cast by the street lamps, the town was in darkness.

Rows of buildings stretched to the east and west, the newer ones of brick but many of wood. Most of these had second floor offices or apartments and a few had third floor sections. At ground level, raised boardwalks separated buildings from the wide dirt road. Shops were locked, their awnings rolled up for the night. Telephone poles topped with crossbeams and glass transistors extended down Main Street in both directions.

Directly across from Fletcher House stood the recently constructed town hall. Azur knew that, as in modern Providence Crossing, the beautiful building contained municipal offices and an acoustically wonderful playhouse. In this earlier period, it also would have fire and police departments and a gaol.

Accustomed to seeing it elegantly displayed as the solitary queen in Victoria Park, Azur was surprised to find the town hall mostly hidden in its surroundings. There were several businesses fronting Main Street including a candy shop, a harness maker and a carriage business. Between the shops and the town hall loomed a large hotel, Johnson House.

Suddenly Azur felt prickles along the back of her neck and down her arms. Her gaze was drawn to an amber glow surrounding the base of a street lamp in front of the candy shop. The amber aura was emitted by a lanky green figure leaning against the lamp post and staring up at her. Azur knew at once what it was, one of the psychic vampires of which Mavis had warned her. A Faefume.

Abruptly she moved from the window and sat trembling on the bed. When the door unexpectedly opened, she jumped up, fearing the worst. But it was only the cleaning girl from the bar.

Unaware of the timerider's presence, the girl removed her apron and shift and tossed them on the chair before sitting on the bed to remove shoes and stockings. Then still clad in bloomers and chemise, she flung herself exhausted into bed.

Although disappointed that she would not have the comfort of the bed for the night, Azur was relieved to have human company. Weary from her own traumatic day, she removed her shawl from the peg and spread it upon the floor. After removed her boots, she stretched out on the shawl and tried to pull some of it over herself for warmth.

It was still dark when the maid arose to begin another long day. She lit a candle from a matchstick and carried the ewer out into the hall. Within minutes she returned, poured water into the basin from the ewer, retrieved a bar of soup from the wash stand's lower shelf, washed face and underarms. She splashed on water, dried herself with a towel, and donned the clothing set out the previous night placed on the chair. Then she carefully carried the basin of wash water out to the hall and returned shortly to return it to the wash stand. After running a brush through her hair, she tied it back with a black ribbon. Hastily she tidied the bed, blew out the candle and departed to begin her chores.

When she felt certain that the woman would not soon return, Azur rose from the floor and lay down upon the bed, sighing as her head sank into the feather pillow. Almost immediately she dozed off, not waking until the sounds of voices mingled with wagon wheels and horses drifted through the window. Initially confused, she sat up and took in the unfamiliar surroundings.

"Oh my God, I'm here by myself," she whispered to the empty room. "What am I to do?"

The timerider took some deep breaths to calm herself. Then she rose, donned boots over her stockinged feet, snapped on the waist bag and wrapped her shawl around her shoulders.

"I can do this," she assured herself, willing herself to believe.

Grabbing her duffle bag, she descended the stairs, crossed the lobby, and exited the hotel. Around her, people went about their early morning activities. No one glanced in her direction as she walked along the boardwalk, peering in store windows. She returned to the station, hoping to find someone who could provide information about the midnight train.

The depot was already busy with people rushing here and there. Travellers stood along the platform and when a train stopped alongside, loaders and baggage handlers sprang into action. A smiling conductor assisted passengers as they boarded. Azur tried unsuccessfully to communicate with the many people milling about. No one seemed aware of her existence.

Eventually she crossed the street and turned east at the Anderson House, walking purposefully past shops of brick and frame. Intent on her next destination, she scarcely noticed shop keepers lowering awnings and sweeping entrance ways in readiness for their first customers of the day.

When she reached Oil Street, Azur turned south at the Vaughn Block. She paused to admire a little bank, its board and batten exterior painted red. In modern Providence Crossing, this same small building, still called the Little Red Bank, was a white stuccoed law office with crimson trim.

The timerider proceeded south on Oil Street and turned left on Henry Street before coming to a halt on the dirt road. With Warren Avenue in sight, her heart began to race. She was entering the residential area known as Crescent Park. She was almost there!

And there it was - her beautiful home! A large square light brick house in traditional Italianate Village style, it had tall multi-paned windows, a low angled roof and boxed cornices with brackets. Ornate gingerbread adorned the verandah which wrapped around the home's front and side.

The timerider was relieved to find it comfortingly recognizable, its variances charming and genteel. Whereas the home in which she had been raised was bright and open, in this earlier era it possessed an air of darker mystique. The verandah was swaddled protectively in ivy and a stain glass atrium enclosed the front entrance. Shrubs and autumn flowers surrounded a gas lamp on the manicured front lawn.

Before approaching the house, Azur continued along the tree-lined road, following it as it curved towards the green common laid out for lawn games and tennis. Set back from the road, elegant Gothic and Italianate homes fronted by large verandahs displayed pillars and latticework. To the back of the houses, oil wells pumped, horses softly snorted in cozy barns, and outhouses stood unabashedly midst shrubbery, tangled vines and heavy-headed sunflowers at the end of garden trails.

With a lightened heart, Azur returned to the house on Warren. She wandered around the back of the property admiring winding stone pathways, ivy-covered trellises, decorative bird houses, sculpted shrubs and winter-readied garden beds. A landscaped terrace descended a lengthy slope to where Bear Creek flowing languidly on its journey through tangled brush and marshy clearings.

Unexpectedly the timerider found herself consumed with homesickness. It seemed that she had been away from Providence Crossing forever instead of mere hours. This place, though beautiful, was not her home. Her grandparents were not here to greet her warmly. Strangers lived in the neighbouring houses. Dejectedly, she entered an ornamental gazebo nestled amid rose bushes where she sat upon a stone bench and wept inconsolably.

Seven

"Why are you crying?" asked a child's voice nearby.

The timerider looked up to see a small boy watching her from outside the gazebo. She brushed at the tears on her cheeks and smiled at the child.

"Do you live here?" she asked him.

"Yes."

"What's your name?"

"Malcolm Isbister. I'm three," he said holding up three fingers in explanation. "James is also three."

"Oh, you have a twin brother."

The boy nodded.

"My Papa died," he said. "Were you crying because your Papa died?"

"No, but I haven't seen him for a long time," she answered honestly. "I'm sorry to hear that your Papa died."

"And John's gone away to school so now there's just Mama and my sisters and my other brothers living here," said the boy.

"Malcolm!" called a female voice from the house. "Where are you?"

"Your mother's calling you," said Azur when the boy seemed in no hurry to respond.

"That's not Mama," said the boy. "That's Charlene."

"One of your sisters?"

"No. Charlene helps Mama."

A teenage girl wearing a blue tunic over a white blouse and ankle-length grey skirt briskly crossed the lawn and grasped the boy's arm. "I haven't time for this today, Malcolm," she said crossly,

"Bye Lady," said Malcolm unperturbed, looking back over his shoulder at Azur as he was escorted to the house.

"Such an imagination!" said Charlene. "Wish I had time for pretend games."

The timerider remained in the gazebo until restlessness overtook her. It was still early morning, hours before she was to meet the midnight train with her friend and the doctor on board. She refused to contemplate the thought that they might not arrive at all.

Finally, she stood, stretched and slowly approached the house. Peering through a side window, she saw the family sitting around a large table engaged in animated conversation. She quietly opened the back door and entered the kitchen where the family breakfasted.

Besides the table at which the family ate, there was a pastry table along one wall with metal drawers for flour and sugar. The room also contained a coal stove, an ice box and a hutch with built-in bread box, cutting board and spice racks.

Seven people sat around the table, a woman in her late thirties, two teenage girls, a boy somewhat younger, a girl younger still, and the little twin boys. The woman and older girls wore black. A family in mourning, noted Azur.

"Mama, why are you going to Guelph again?" asked Malcolm.

"Please don't whine, Malcolm. I told you Aunt Gail is ailing, and I must see to her."

"How long will you be gone?" asked the boy's twin.

"Only a fortnight or so, James," said Mama.

"Oooh!" moaned James. "Maude and Mabel are mean to us when you're not here."

"Not mean enough," muttered the younger of the teenage girls, glaring at the little boys.

"I heard that, Mabel," said their mother. "I'm counting on you to be nice to the little ones when I'm away. Oh, and Maude, don't forget to have Alice and William do their piano practicing."

"Yes, Mama," said Maude despondently.

"Every day," insisted her mother.

"Yes, Mama," sighed the girl.

"I wish old Mrs. Hammond wasn't going to be nosing around while you're gone," said Mabel.

"Don't be disrespectful of your elders," said Mama. "Besides, Mrs. Hammond is not old. She's still in her forties."

"Papa was forty-five when he died," said the oldest of the three boys.

"Yes, William. And fortunate we are that Mr. Hammond and Mr. Sanson offered to be the guardians of you children after your dear father passed."

"We have a mother. Why do we need guardians?" complained Maude.

"Widows need men looking after their affairs," said William.

"Mr. Sanson is a widower," noted Mabel. "Do his children have guardians because his wife passed?"

"It doesn't work that way," said her mother.

"Mama *needs* Mr. Hammond and Mr. Sanson to help her manage the Inn & Bakery, don't you Mama?" said William.

"Our John wanted to drop out of school to manage it," Maude reminded him.

"But Mr. Hammond wouldn't hear of it," sighed Mama. "He insisted that John finish law school first. Fortunate we are that George Murray has been able to take over the baking at the inn. He was always your father's right hand man."

"Look, Mama! There's the lady I saw at the gazebo," said Malcolm, suddenly spotting the timerider standing in the kitchen.

Azur was now aware that both twins as well as Mabel were looking at her with interest. Three of these children are sensointuitive, she realized.

"No make believe, Malcolm," said his mother sternly. "You're getting too old to be talking like that!"

"You see her, don't you, Mabel?" persisted Malcolm.

"No she doesn't!" said Mama. "Do you want to have your sister branded as peculiar?"

"Don't you mean witch?" asked Mabel quietly.

"See! That's what comes of all this silly talk," said Maude. "Make him stop, Mama, or I'll lose all my friends."

"Good heavens, children! It's time for school. Kiss me good-bye and get your school bags and lunches from Charlene. William Hammond will be here any minute to take me to the train!"

The four oldest children dutifully rose from the table and kissed their mother.

"Don't worry about a thing, Mama," said Maude. "I'll keep everyone in line. Give our love to Aunt Gail."

"Be nice to Mrs. Hammond. And help Charlene by tidying up your things," admonished Mama.

"Hurry back," said Alice. "I'll miss you so much!" She began to cry.

"I'll be back soon, Alice. Stop crying or you'll make me feel worse," said her mother.

As they made their way to the door, Mabel brushed against Azur. "You can read in the library until I get home," she whispered. "Then I'll come and talk to you."

Azur smiled at the girl gratefully.

The children had barely left for school when the doorbell rang. Malcolm ran to open it. "Mama," he yelled. "Mrs. Hammond is here already!"

"Shush, Malcolm," his mother scolded. "No shouting in the house." To herself she muttered, *Eliza already thinks I have a bunch of hooligans.*

Eliza Hammond was indeed already standing in the hall. "I wanted to be here when you headed out, Margaret," she said, "to reassure you that everything is in good hands. William is out front waiting for you. He'll help you with your luggage."

"You're both too kind, Eliza," said Margaret Isbister.

"Not at all."

"I hope you don't feel obliged to spend a lot of time here, Eliza. The little boys are fine with Charlene while the others are at school, and the girls are quite capable of managing things the rest of the time. I'm actually more concerned about the Inn & Bakery."

"You needn't fret about that either, Margaret. My William and George Sanson will both be keeping an eye on things there until you return."

"Well I guess I'm off then. Come kiss me goodbye, boys. Charlene, don't let them out of your sight for a moment!"

"No, Ma'am," said the servant girl.

As soon as the carriage bearing Margaret Isbister pulled away, Eliza Hammond took it upon herself to tour the house.

"Why are you walking around our house?" asked James.

"Have you been taught no manners, child?" asked the woman. "I want to be certain that, when your mother returns home, everything looks the same as now."

Azur had been watching the flurry of farewell activities from where she sat half way up the front stairs. She remained there observing Eliza Hammond thoroughly inspecting the upstairs and downstairs of the Isbister home. "What a nosy do-gooder you are," she muttered, at which the twins laughed uproariously.

"Oops, forgot you could hear me," said the timerider.

"What are you being so silly about?" queried Eliza, eying the boys severely.

"Nothing, Mrs. Hammond," said the boys in unison, trying not to giggle.

"Make sure you do what Charlene tells you, and mind your sisters once they get home. Tell them to telephone me if there are any problems."

"There won't be any problems," said Malcolm.

"Malcolm and James! Are you listening?"

"Yes, Mrs. Hammond."

"Don't forget to have your sisters telephone me from the inn if they need me for anything," she repeated.

"Yes, Mrs. Hammond."

"Perhaps you should run outside to play while I speak with Charlene."

"Yes, Mrs. Hammond."

"And don't leave the yard!"

"No, Mrs. Hammond." The little boys eagerly rushed from the house.

"Do you have all your canning done for the winter?" Eliza asked the servant who was standing anxiously nearby.

"Yes, Ma'am. We finished that last week."

"Lots of vegetables in your root cellar?"

"Yes, Ma'am."

"Anything left in your garden?"

"Just a few beets and potatoes, Ma'am."

"You'll be seeing to those, of course."

"Yes, Ma'am."

"Goodness me. There's William back for me already. I'd best be on my way. Will you be alright until I return tomorrow, Charlene?"

"Yes, Ma'am," said the servant.

"I noticed there are a lot of things that need attending to."

"Yes, Ma'am."

"I don't know how poor Margaret manages," muttered Eliza Hammond as she exited through the front door.

Eight

After William and Eliza Hammond drove away in their horse drawn carriage, Azur decided to follow Mabel's suggestion to relax in the library. She moved from room to room wondering which one the Isbisters used for reading.

The house was built on a side plan with the front stairway just within the door on the left leading upstairs and the living room on the right. The front hall, carpeted in pale blue, had gold and white provincial wallpaper. Crystal chandeliers along with brass and glass doorknobs added elegance throughout the house. The living room was graced with an oriental rug, grand piano, sofas, high backed chairs and a small cherry table.

Distinguished from the kitchen, the dining room contained a formal dining suite and a grandfather clock. A charming bay window alcove adjoined the dining room and opened onto the porch. There were two wood-panelled sunrooms.

Azur now entered a lovely room with beamed ceiling, book cases and a fireplace - the Isbister library. In the present time, this room also had a television and was Bram's den. How lonely it seems without my grandfather, she thought longingly. She selected a book randomly, settled back into a wingchair upholstered in satin brocade and, with feet propped on a matching ottoman, closed her eyes to rest.

When Mabel Isbister returned home from school later in the day, she found the timerider asleep in the library. She was standing there quietly when her twin brothers burst into the room.

"We knew she was there but Charlene wouldn't let us come in here," said James.

"Of course not!" said Mabel. "You're never allowed in the library."

Wakened by the conversation, Azur opened her eyes. "Have I been sleeping long?" she asked.

"All day!" said Malcolm. "Will you play with us now?"

"She's coming upstairs with me," said Mabel. "Go outside and play."

"Go outside and play, go outside and play. That's all everybody says to us!"

"Ask Maude to read to you."

"What if she says, No?"

"Tell her you'll tell Mama. Or Mrs. Hammond," said Mabel with a smile.

The boys ran off and Mabel beckoned the timerider to follow her up the winding front stairs. She led Azur through four bedrooms in the front part of the upstairs.

"Mama sleeps here," she said, indicating the largest front bedroom. "You can stay in this room until she gets back."

"That's very kind of you," said Azur. "Perhaps I will."

"Maude sleeps here, Alice and I sleep in this room, and the twins sleep in this smaller room," said Mabel, continuing the tour.

She then took Azur down a step to a back section which had a fifth bedroom and a bathroom. As in modern times, the back stairway descended from there to the kitchen. Azur noticed that, while there was running water for the tub and sink, the bathroom had no toilet. It really was a room intended for bathing.

"Does Charlene sleep here?" Azur asked, indicating the back bedroom.

"No. She goes home at night. This is William's room."

"Oh, of course, I forgot William. So where does Charlene live?"

"She lives at the Isbister Inn & Bakery, but she's here with us from six in the morning until nine at night."

"That's the inn your family owns."

"Yes. Charlene's parents, Mr. and Mrs. Murray, live on the premises and operate it for Mama. One of the domestics, Nelly, also lives there. Then, of course, there are several lodgers – six or seven, I believe."

"And your mother helps at the inn," noted Azur.

"Mama *supervises* the inn, but of course, ladies don't actually do that kind of work. When Papa was alive, he loved to bake, so he pretty much ran the bakery."

"I overheard the conversation this morning about the guardians you've had since your father died. Does it bother you?"

"Not usually. Mr. Hammond and Mr. Sanson help Mama with the financial end of things. Other than that, we don't see a lot of them. We could certainly have worse guardians."

"Mrs. Hammond was here this morning," Azur informed the girl.

"Well I could have predicted that! She doesn't have any children of her own - although her niece lives with her - so she likes to come over here and tell Mama how undisciplined we are. She thinks her meddling is helpful."

"Does your mother mind?"

"Mama and Mrs. Hammond are friends. Mama says it's not our place to criticize someone who does her favours."

"What about the Sansons?"

"Mr. Sanson is a widower so he's pretty busy with his own family. He and his wife had seven children before Mrs. Sanson died."

"Good heavens! Are they all at home?"

"Just three of them. His oldest son is a doctor off in British Columbia and two of his daughters are married. Then there's my brother John's friend, Alexander, who's at veterinary school."

"And the ones still at home?"

"The youngest boy is only thirteen, but the other two are in their twenties. Ellen is a teacher and Thomas is a blacksmith."

"It must be hard for all of you since your father died," sympathized Azur.

"We miss him so much," sighed the girl. "But mostly we're able to manage."

"Mabel! Where are you?" called Maude from downstairs.

"I have to go now and help with supper," said Mabel. "Stay in my room and I'll come and talk with you after we finish eating."

True to her word, Mabel returned shortly after the family rose from their evening meal. Her little sister, Alice was with her. "You can talk to me or ask me questions," she said, smiling at the timerider.

"You can tell me a story," said Alice, unaware that her sister was communicating with a third person.

"How old is Alice?" asked Azur.

"Alice is six, William is ten, the twins are three, Maude is sixteen, I'm fourteen and John is twenty-one. He's a law student."

"That's not a story," laughed Alice.

"Oh, I thought it was," teased Mabel. "What's your name and how old are you?" she asked the timerider.

"You just said my name and how old I am," giggled Alice.

"My name is Azur Moonstorey and I'm nineteen," Azur told Mabel. "I'm here to find my sister who came here a year ago. I'm a sensointuitive – like you."

"Good heavens," said Mabel. "I'm not at all like you. I'm just an ordinary girl who's never been farther than Guelph or Toronto."

"It's pretty hard to explain," admitted Azur, deciding against speaking of time travel and mutants. "Have you met other people like me before?"

"You mean ghost visitors or shadow people that only certain folk can see?"

"Yes."

"Last year I saw a girl in our back garden around this time of year."

"Did you talk to her?"

"No. By the time I made it outside, she was gone."

"That probably was Hilma," said Azur sadly.

"What girl?" asked Alice, listening with puzzlement to her sister's side of the conversation with the timerider.

"Just a girl," Mabel told her sister.

"Have you ever heard strange stories or rumours about the visitors?"

"I've heard that sometimes ghost visitors disappear before the Hallowmas train returns for them. I think something bad must happen to them."

"What happens to them?" asked Alice.

"I was talking nonsense," said Mabel to the little girl. "Mama doesn't like me telling you scary stories."

"Because I have bad dreams?" asked Alice.

"How should I go about finding my sister?" asked Azur.

"I really don't know. I'm sorry."

"You know I have bad dreams, silly!" said Alice.

"When you have bad dreams, you can come to me and I'll protect you." Mabel looked meaningfully at Azur, then smiled at her sister so the little girl would think the comment was for her.

"You're a good protector," said Alice, snuggling against Mabel.

"Have you heard of Vapourlea?" Azur asked Mabel.

"No. What is it?"

"It's a place. Here, actually. It's the invisible dimension of Prosper Station where bad things happen."

"Enough bad things happen in the real Prosper Station," said Mabel. "There are robberies and train accidents and nitroglycerin explosions. On top of that, the streets aren't safe even in the daytime with all the rough men around."

"Are you going to tell me a story about the men who drink in the hotels at night with the painted women?" asked Alice hopefully.

"That would be a silly story," said Mabel.

"I'm hoping to meet some friends at the station tonight," said Azur.

"Ghost visitors?"

"Yes. We call ourselves timeriders."

"Be very careful," said Mabel to Azur.

Alice laughed with glee. "Yes, yes. Tell me a story about ghosts," she said.

"I'm going to your mother's room now," said Azur, leaving the girls to their story-telling.

DAY 3

October 24

Nine

Alone in Margaret Isbister's unoccupied bedroom, Azur rocked back and forth, back and forth on the matron's padded wicker rocker willing the rhythm to numb her tempestuous emotions. At frequent intervals she checked Bram's pocket watch wanting, while at the same time dreading, for the hands to move closer to midnight. The timerider's grandfather had thoughtfully handed her the timepiece prior to her departure, knowing that her digital watch would be of little use in a nineteenth century dimension.

For a while, the commotion of the Isbister children preparing for bed ran a distracting counterpoint through Azur's anxiety. But soon the house was quiet with the exception of occasional sighs, snuffles and snores from the young sleepers upstairs or a downstairs thump where Charlene was tidying up.

All at once a crescendo of wailing brought Azur to her feet. She followed Maude and Mabel into the twins' room and was soon joined by Charlene carrying a lamp from downstairs.

"I have an earache," cried James. "I want Mama!"

"It's okay," soothed Maude. "We'll look after you." She ordered Charlene to heat water and Mabel to get a basin, cloth and oil. Within moments, Mabel returned with the items requested of her.

"What kind of oil is it?" Azur asked.

"It's a mixture of essential oils of lavender, chamomile and thyme," explained the girl, holding up a small glass bottle with a narrow neck and stopper.

"I know what kind of oil it is," snapped Maude, thinking that her sister was addressing her.

"Sorry," said Azur to Mabel who rolled her eyes.

"It hurts! It hurts!" screamed James, tears streaming down his blotchy face.

"Charlene, where are you?!" shouted Maude.

The servant breathlessly climbed the stairs bearing a steaming kettle and poured its contents into the basin. Holding the bottle carefully by its neck, Mabel lowered it into the hot water for a few seconds before handing it to Maude.

The older girl tested the temperature of the oil on her wrist, and satisfied, tilted the bottle to drip warm oil into the boy's ear. While she did this, Mabel immersed a cloth in the basin, wrung it out and handed it to her sister.

"This will make you feel better," soothed Maude, applying the warm compress.

"It still hurts!" moaned James. "Get the doctor."

"Mama would never bring the doctor out at night for an earache," said Mabel.

"Call Mrs. Hammond then," cried the boy. "She said to call her."

"I could call her from the inn's telephone," offered Charlene.

"We don't need Mrs. Hammond," said Maude almost in tears herself.

Azur watched in dismay as the little boy thrashed about. She approached the bed and put her hands gently on both sides of his face to comfort him.

"Lie still, James, and you'll feel better," she said.

Almost immediately her hands became tingly and she felt heat radiating from the boy into her arms. She pulled away in alarm, fearing she was harming the young patient. But James stopped crying and smiled up at her.

"Thank you, Lady," he said. "The breeze made my ear cool."

"He's delirious," said Charlene in alarm.

"Are you alright, James?" asked a concerned Maude.

"He's fine," announced Malcolm as his brother, a smile on his lips, dozed off. "Everybody go to bed. I'm tired."

With a few hesitant backward glances, the sisters and the servant tiptoed from the room. Maude and Mabel went back to their beds and Charlene to the lower floor.

Bemused by the experience, Azur bent over the sleeping boy and blew Malcolm a kiss before returning to the widow's room.

"Did I do that, Zhiab?" she whispered.

Yes. A good beginning.

"Are you going to stay with me?"

I'm present when you need me.

"Don't leave! I'm terrified to go out on those dark streets alone."

Depart with the servant and walk with her until she reaches her residence. Then continue on to the depot and wait there for the midnight train.

Somewhat reassured, Azur picked up her shawl and tiptoed down to the kitchen where Charlene was completing her final tasks for the day. At nine o'clock, the girl slipped into her coat and snuffed out the last of the lamps. She locked the back door, placed the key under a flower pot and set off down the dimly lit streets unaware of the timerider at her side.

At Main Street, they crossed to the boardwalk on the north side and began to walk westward. When Charlene halted and looked around questioningly, Azur sensed that the girl had heard her footsteps on the planked walkway. She quickly stepped down onto the road, keeping pace with the servant.

As they passed the Normandy Hotel, a woman with rouged lips stood in the doorway, smiling seductively at passersby. The low cut of her tautly laced bodice emphasized her ample bosom.

"Care to make some extra money?" she called out to the servant girl. "The men like young things," she teased.

"My day's long enough, Savannah" said Charlene with a tired smile.

A few doors further along, the girl reached the Inn & Bakery and disappeared inside. Alone now, Azur began to walk quickly toward the station. A sinister chuckle made her gasp even before the hazy green form appeared in her path. When the timerider moved to the side, the form slid sideways with her, blocking her way.

"Zhiab," she called softly.

Taunting laughter from the misty shape was the sole response. Desperately, the timerider put her hands in front of her and pushed ahead. The form faded away and Azur ran frantically to the station pursued by eerie laughter.

At the depot, Azur moved unseen among passengers and workmen, taking comfort in human bustle. Labourers pushed carts stacked with parcels and crates here and there. In one large section, horses pulling wagon loads of crude oil waited in line. As each wagon pulled up, oil barrels were hefted onto the ground.

Whistles, bells and squealing brakes announced the arrival of a train which pulled up to the platform, emitting blasts of steam. Workers sprang into action to load and unload the numerous freight cars while a conductor and baggage handler escorted people from a single passenger car.

Some passengers were greeted by drivers who took their luggage and assisted them into handsome carriages. Most passengers, however, walked to their homes or lodgings toting their own belongings.

By the time the train left for its next destination, only a few workers remained at the rail yard. Azur climbed the steps to the wooden station where lights flickered invitingly from within. She entered the building and, to her surprise, the same porter who had carried her baggage on the previous night was bent over papers at a desk.

"You've come to meet your friends," he noted, looking up. "Their baggage is still here waiting for them."

"You can see me," noted Azur.

He nodded. "Did you find suitable lodgings?" he asked.

"Yes," she replied without elaborating.

The porter returned to his papers and Azur sat down on a bench to wait. After an interminable interval, she heard a far off rumbling growing steadily louder and closer. She shivered in fear when Steam Engine 330 sent out eerie blasts and whistles as it roared toward the depot. Trembling, she forced herself to descend to the passenger platform, watching anxiously as the pinpoint of light became larger and brighter. Two long whistles and a short one followed by clanging bells, hisses and snorts announced the arrival of the iron monster.

Steps were lowered from the passenger car to the platform and the conductor in uniform of navy blue and polished brass stood in the doorway. Scarcely breathing, Azur waited for passengers to appear. Finally, a solitary figure stood beside the conductor.

"Dilly! Dilly!" shouted Azur, running to the platform to greet her friend.

"Thank heavens you're here," said Dillian. "They didn't let XT on the train again and I was so frightened that I wouldn't find you."

The young women hugged each other in affection and relief.

"Your luggage, Miss," said the porter, holding Dillian's duffle bag.

"Thank you," said Dilly, reaching for her bag.

"The young man missed the train again, I see."

"Not by choice," said Dilly.

Ten

"Where are we going?" asked Dilly, one arm companionably through that of her friend's, the other toting her duffle bag.

"To my house in Crescent Park," replied Azur as they hastened along Main Street. "The Isbister family lives there."

"Will we be able to get inside?"

"I know where they hide the key. We can stay in Mrs. Isbister's room for a couple of days because she's visiting her sister in Guelph."

"Will anyone know we're there?"

"Yes, three of the kids seem to have acquired the mutation, and they're very welcoming to timeriders."

"I need to spend some time in the Tecumseh House," said Dilly.

"Is that where your great-great grandfather was killed?"

"Yes, and where he allegedly murdered the woman."

"We'll scope it out in daylight when the town is less spooky. Now tell me about last night. Were Bram and Mavis shocked to see you?"

"We didn't want to alarm them so we didn't go there."

"You went to your Mom's?"

Dilly shook her head. "She'd have asked too many questions."

"So where did you go?"

"XT's apartment."

"Oh."

"Azur! You're jealous," exclaimed Dilly.

"Why would I be jealous? I only met him two days ago."

"Well, he's charming, handsome, sensitive, to say nothing of considerate. Can you believe he was going to change the bedding for me until I insisted that he needn't bother because I would sleep on the couch?"

"Did you tell him you were engaged?"

"See, you are jealous. And, yes, I told him about Graeme. And, yes, he slept in his bed and I on the couch. Then we had to stay inside all day so no one would see us. The television was on but we couldn't focus on anything because we were too freaked about you and the train. And for a doctor, the man had nothing fit to eat in the place so we microwaved popcorn. Are you still envious?"

"You're crazy, Dil," laughed Azur, nudging her friend.

"No wonder I was so hungry on that ghastly train. In spite of my terror, I ate enough of those little hors d'oeuvre things to equal a full course dinner."

"Did you sleep on the train?"

"Funny you should ask. I slept most of the trip. Did you?"

"Yeah. I think it was the tea."

"Coulda been those yummy little cakes."

"Did XT try to catch the train?"

"Of course he *tried*, but the conductor helped me on board and poor XT got left behind."

"It doesn't look as if he'll make it here," said Azur. "Just as well. He's not a Senso."

"Azur!" whispered Dilly, "What's that?"

Absorbed in conversation, the women had not noticed the smirking green figures lined up along both sides of Main Street near the Vaughn Block.

"Keep walking," said Azur through clenched teeth.

The line of green figures floated towards them, quickly enclosing them in a spinning orb which elongated into a fluorescent funnel of marbleized green and amber hues.

"Run, Azur! Run!" yelled Dilly who, while still clutching her bag, pulled her friend towards the funnel mouth.

They ran until their legs felt like rubber, their lungs burned and their breathing came in ragged gasps. By now the funnel had spun itself into an endless tunnel with no opening visible on either end.

"When I have fears that I may cease to be…When I have fears that I may cease to be," chanted Dilly breathlessly as they stumbled onward. "When I have fears that I may cease to be… When I have fears that I may cease to be."

"We're trapped by the Faefumes and you're quoting Keats?"

"Those words were on a piece of paper in his coat pocket," she panted.

"Your great-great…"

"Yes. I hoped it was a spell."

"Zhiab, we need you," whispered Azur when the women stopped to catch their breath.

Dilly glanced at her friend in puzzlement.

"Zhiab!" called Azur.

They're testing you.

"I can't do this!" she screamed.

Sinister jeers and taunting laughter swirled through the tunnel.

"That does it!" shouted Azur, enraged. She flung her arms out to the side, fingers splayed. Energy coursed through her being, exploding from her fingertips. Groans and howls echoed through the tunnel as its walls faded into wisps which floated off into the darkness.

"How did you do that?" asked Dillian in amazement.

"I don't know," answered Azur truthfully.

"Incredible. After all that running we're still near the intersection of Main and Oil," noted Dilly taking in her surroundings. "Oh, Azur! How beautifully quaint this town is!"

"Let's get to the house while we still can," said Azur.

The women walked quickly until they stood in front of the Isbister home.

"The Crescent looks lovely in lamplight," said Dilly. "Even the dirt road has a certain charm."

"How can you be thinking of esthetics at a time like this?"

"Look at all the stars. It's so beautiful I could cry!"

"Keep on walking or you'll *be* crying," said her friend.

"Azur, the moon is in its first quarter. Your grandmother would place some importance on this."

"It's the week of waxing moon magic, a cycle of constructive enchantment."

"Meaning?"

"Sensos are supposed to be able to draw upon lunar power to enhance love, friendship, courage, success and health," supplied Azur.

"Perfect!" enthused Dilly. "Do you know how to do that?"

"Dillian, let's talk about all this after we're safely inside."

Azur retrieved the key from under the flower pot and unlocked the back door. Once inside, she and Dillian tiptoed through the house and up the front staircase to Margaret Isbister's room. Exhausted, Azur removed her boots and flung herself upon the bed.

"There's room for you," she invited Dilly, patting one side of the bed.

"I'm not at all tired, so I'll just sit in the rocking chair," said her friend.

"Your sleep on the train must have been refreshing."

"You jest," said Dilly. "But it is strange. Even after all that running from the green things, I feel alert."

"Overstimulation," muttered Azur sleepily.

"Before you nod off, tell me what's happened so far," insisted Dilly.

Azur gave her friend a summary of her encounters with Zhiab and the Faefumes. She filled her in briefly on the Isbister family and some of the highlights of the town.

"You haven't told me about your powers."

"I wish I had some."

"But you do! You cured the little boy's earache and you pushed away the Faefume on your way to meet me. And you made that terrorizing tunnel disappear."

"I have no idea how any of that happened."

You must learn how to control the powers with which you are gifted.

"Is that Zhiab?" asked Dilly in wonder.

"You heard him?" asked Azur.

"Certainly."

"So how do I learn to control them?" Azur asked the Novapetrol.

After a prolonged silence, Dilly said, "I didn't hear his answer."

"There was no answer, Dillian. Zhiab is very annoying that way."

"He wants you to figure it out for yourself."

"No kidding!"

"Let's figure it out then. When were you able to use your power?"

"Each situation was different."

"Think, girl. What do healing an earache, clearing your path and melting a tunnel have in common?"

"Not much."

"Okay, what did you do in each situation?"

"I used my hands."

"Do something with your hands now."

"Like what?"

"Make me feel sleepy."

Azur moved her arm slowly in the direction of the rocking chair and its occupant, willing her friend to experience enough weariness to quit talking. Nothing happened.

"Something is missing," mused Dillian.

"I'm tired," protested Azur.

"That must be it! You don't have enough energy right now. How were you feeling when you cured the little boy?"

"I wanted his pain to go away," mumbled Azur.

"Compassion," said Dilly thoughtfully. "And what were you feeling when you met the Faefume on the road to the station?"

"Fear, I guess."

"You seemed to go ballistic in the tunnel," noted Dilly.

"I was furious at the jeering and taunting of those repulsive creatures," recalled Azur.

"You were angry. That's it! Emotion gives you the energy to turn on your powers."

Well done, Dillian.

"Thanks, Zhiab."

"It's that simple?" asked Azur.

Turn on your aptitudes, young Senso.

"You said that before," grumbled Azur.

"I think he's saying that practice makes perfect," suggested Dilly *Well put.*

"Don't do your vanishing act yet, Zhiab," said Dilly. "Do I have any powers?"

Indeed you are already demonstrating them.

Eleven

"Who could that be at this hour?" wondered Bram, rising from his first coffee of the morning.

"Okay, okay," he muttered when the knocking persisted while he was making his way to the front door.

Minutes later he returned to the kitchen accompanied by a disheveled visitor.

"XT!" exclaimed Mavis. "What are you doing here?"

"I was rejected by that cursed train. Twice," he said.

"And the girls?" asked Bram anxiously.

"Azur got on the first night and Dillian made it last night."

"Oh, my goodness," said Mavis. "I hope they connected with each other."

"That's why I have to get on that train! You've got to help me," pleaded the doctor.

"For your research?" asked Bram, an edge to his voice.

"That's the last thing I'm thinking about now," protested Xavier Tennyson. "I'm worried about those young women being all alone."

"You're not a Senso, XT," Mavis pointed out. "Even if you managed to board the train and exit at the other end, it wouldn't be safe for you there. And it's quite likely that Azur and Dilly would be invisible to you."

Staring at each other in dismay, the three paid no attention to the sleek silvery blue feline that entered the room and made its way purposefully toward the visitor.

"Mrrroow," said Bleu loudly, rubbing against XT's leg.

"Do *you* have any suggestions?" muttered the man, bending down to scratch the cat behind her ears.

"Where are our manners, Dr. Barkley?" apologized Mavis suddenly realizing that their visitor remained standing. "Have you had breakfast?"

"Not yet."

"Well sit down and have coffee with us and I'll get you something to eat."

"Corn flakes would be fine if you have some."

While XT munched on his cereal and gratefully sipped coffee, Bleu persisted is purring loudly and rubbing against his trouser legs.

"You're being even more intrusive than usual, Bleu," scolded Bram.

"Please help me get on that train," pleaded XT to the Galvinstons.

"I don't see how," replied Mavis.

"Mrrroow," cried the cat, leaping into XT's lap and knocking the spoon from his hand.

"Get down, Bleu!" exclaimed Bram, rising to remove the errant cat from the startled doctor's knees. "What's wrong with you?"

Bleu clung on defiantly, refusing to budge. As Bram, Mavis and XT looked on in amazement, her fur took on a deep blue hue and her eyes became glowing sapphires. Gazing up at XT, she chirped and purred. Then she jumped to the floor and faded back to her usual shade of bluish silver fur with eyes of pale green.

Mavis gazed at the cat thoughtfully. "Are you telling us that XT should not even think about boarding the train?" she asked.

The cat ignored her.

"Bleu, do you think XT *should* board the train?"

The cat rubbed against XT and again her fur changed colour as did her glittering eyes.

"I've never seen the like," said Bram.

XT pulled his chair away from the table and still seated, called to the cat. With a gleeful "Mrrrooow," she jumped upon him and as man and feline touched, a silvery blue aura encased them.

"Do you feel anything?" asked Mavis intrigued.

"Yes I'm all tingly," said XT.

"Do you suppose Bleu's a catalyst?" mused Bram.

"Could she enable a person who is not sensointuitive to cross into another dimension?" wondered Mavis.

"This is wonderful!" exclaimed XT. "Bleu and I can make the trip together. Should we leave now?"

"Slow down, Dr. Barkley. To begin with, it's not midnight, and between now and then, we have a lot of things to consider. Unlike a mutant timerider, you will most likely have physical substance and require nourishment and lodgings. You'll have to hide in plain sight."

"Since many of the town's young professionals and labourers in that period lodged in hotels and boarding houses, XT could do likewise," suggested Bram.

"You'll need nineteenth-century money!" realized Mavis.

"I'm ahead of you there," chuckled XT. "I have a little trove of gold and silver coins and ingots."

"Really?" asked Mavis.

"You don't say!" said Bram.

"They were a gift from my grandfather on my twenty-first birthday. Before I came to Providence Crossing, I transferred half of it from my bank vault at home to a bank in Providence Crossing. I've sewn several of the coins into my clothing."

"Xavier Tennyson, you amaze me!" said Mavis.

"It turns out I was quite naïve though. I thought it would be a simple matter of boarding a train at midnight. I knew nothing of invisible timeriders.

"Well your naivety paid off – at least with the gold and silver," said Bram. "Have you given any thought as to who might buy it?"

"Hopefully, a hotel keeper or a jeweller."

"Sounds probable," admitted Bram. "What do you know about money in nineteenth century Canada?"

"Apparently, coinage was minted for Canada at England's Royal Mint in one, five, ten and twenty-cent pieces along with two-dollar coins. Bank notes were issued in Ottawa in one, two, five-hundred and one-thousand dollar amounts."

"You've done your homework."

"It didn't get me on the train," noted XT ruefully.

The remainder of the day passed in a flurry of activity. XT returned to his apartment to shower and retrieve belongings necessary for the journey. Mavis instructed him, much as she had Azur and Dillian, in what he might expect to encounter in Victorian Prosper. She told him about Faefumes and warned him that, while these might be invisible to him, they would surely see him. When she told him about Novapetrols, it occurred to her that they were blue like the cat in its catalytic form.

"Blue guardians," smiled XT.

As the evening wore on, they discussed various ways of transporting Bleu. In the end, it was decided that the cat would travel in a sling bag that could be worn as a back pack or on a diagonal strap across the front or side.

Shortly before midnight, Bram and Mavis bid Godspeed to the young man.

"I'm getting well-practiced at this," he assured them. With a nod, he set off into the night wearing the sling bag in which Bleu contentedly slept.

As on the previous two occasions, XT entered a brightly lit library. And as before, the light dimmed at midnight transforming to the subdued glow of gas lamps. The walls deepened in colour to their original wood stain while bookshelves transformed into benches.

Once again XT claimed a return ticket.

"Your luggage, Sir?" asked the baggage handler.

"It went on ahead," said XT.

"Shall I take your pack then?" said the handler, reaching for the sling bag.

"Thanks, I'll hang on to this," replied XT.

He followed the man out to the boarding platform and waited anxiously for the train's arrival. Heralding its approach through a crescendo of rumbles and wailing, Steam Engine 330 sped towards the station. It drew up to the platform with clanging bells, screeching brakes and blasts of steam.

Feeling motion inside the sling bag, XT peered in and observed that Bleu's fur stood on end.

"It's okay, girl," he said, giving the cat a reassuring pat.

Magnificent in navy with trim of braid and brass, the conductor appeared at the coach door.

"All aboard," he shouted to the sole passenger.

XT climbed the steps and entered the empty coach. Relieved to be finally inside the train, he chose a window seat and sank into leather luxury placing the bag on the adjoining seat. No sooner was he seated than the train lurch forward, pushing him against the lace-covered back as it departed from the station.

"Your ticket, Sir," said the conductor pleasantly.

As he returned the punched ticket to XT, he glanced into the bag. "I'm afraid animals are not allowed in the coach car," he said. "I'll just take this to the baggage car for you."

Before XT had a chance to resist, a hissing blue feline leapt from the bag. Snarling and hissing, ears flattened against its head, back arched and fur wildly on end, it faced the conductor.

"It seems to want to stay with you," said the conductor stepping away from the seat. "Be so kind as to return it to its bag, Sir, and I'll return shortly with your tea."

Twelve

"There's someone downstairs," whispered Dilly.

"Probably Charlene," mumbled Azur sleepily.

"The servant? But it's only six o'clock."

"I *thought* I heard voices," said Mabel, entering the room in her nightgown. "I was up checking on the twins."

"Mabel, this is my friend, Dillian. I hope you don't mind that I invited her here for the night."

"I was hoping that that you'd find your friend and bring her here," smiled the girl. "Glad to make your acquaintance, Dillian."

"Nice to meet you, Mabel," said the visitor. "I appreciate your hospitality."

"We were wondering if we heard Charlene downstairs," said Azur.

"I hope so. She has to prepare breakfast and make our lunches for school," replied Mabel. "She never seems to get all her work done."

"She has a long day," noted Dilly.

"Not really," said Mabel. "Mama lets her leave at nine each night instead of ten like most people do. She only stays later if there's an evening social, and then she sleeps over because it's late by the time the guests leave. Of course, we haven't had any parties since Papa died."

"How many days a week does Charlene work?" asked Dilly.

"Why every day, of course." Mabel laughed at the absurdity of the question before adding, "But she gets two hours off on

Sunday mornings to attend church. And every afternoon - unless we have company over - she has two hours to amuse herself as she wishes."

"Does everyone work seven days a week?"

"Labourers and clerks get one day off," explained the girl. "Is it not the same where you come from?"

"We usually get two days off a week," said Azur without elaboration. "I hope you don't find our questions intrusive."

"Not at all," said Mabel. "It's nice to have someone like you take an interest in my boring life."

"Do you mind me asking when your father died and how long you're required to wear black?" asked Azur.

"Papa died in the spring," said the girl, tears welling in her eyes.

"I'm sorry," sympathized Dilly.

"Did you know the Queen is still wearing black although Prince Albert died years ago?"

"She must have loved him a lot," said Dilly.

"Oh, she did!" sighed Mabel. "To answer your question, Mama said that Maude and I can start wearing our regular clothes when she gets back from Guelph. I'm not sure how long Mama will stay in mourning. At least a year, I should expect."

"What are you doing in Mama's room?" asked Alice, standing in the bedroom doorway.

"Alice! You startled me," said Mabel.

"Well, what *are* you doing?"

"I was just thinking about Mama and Papa," replied the older girl. "Let's go back to bed for a few more minutes before we have to get dressed."

The timeriders remained in Margaret Isbister's room discussing their plans for the day. They decided to tour the town, hoping to unearth some clues about finding Hilma. They would also stop in at the Tecumseh House where Dilly's ancestor died.

Before leaving for school, Mabel ran up the stairs to say goodbye to her visitors. "If you look out the window in a couple of minutes, you'll see the Moncrieff children," she said. "We always walk to school together. The tallest boy is George. He's one year older than me and so handsome!"

She walked to the window, then whispered, "Oh, come here! There's Mrs. Moncrieff and her sister, Minnie Thompson, driving by in their carriage. I wonder where they're going at this hour."

"That's Charlotte?" asked Dilly excitedly.

"How do you know that Minnie's real name is Charlotte?" asked Mabel.

"She becomes notable in the town's history," explained Azur.

Mabel looked puzzled. "Well she is engaged to one of the town's wealthiest oilmen, Jake Englehart, and their wedding will be spectacular!"

And she'll have a hospital named after her in the future, thought Azur.

After the children disappeared down the street, Azur and Dilly tiptoed down the front stairs and passed Charlene on her hands and knees scrubbing the hall floor. The timeriders glanced at each other and rolled their eyes.

"Where are you going?" asked Malcolm, walking out from the kitchen to eye the visitors expectantly.

"Does it look like I'm going anywhere?" asked Charlene brusquely. "Go play with James and don't step on this floor!"

"We're going downtown," Azur told the boy.

"Can we come with you?" he asked.

Azur smiled and shook her head and Malcolm turned away, head and shoulders drooped in dramatized dejection.

When the timeriders reached the business section of town, they found that, even at this early hour, the town was bustling.

"Thank heavens it's not creepy in daylight," said Dilly.

"It's actually kind of charming despite the oily smell, don't you think?" asked Azur as they walked westward along the boardwalk. Cyclists pedalled by on bicycles while horses plodded along pulling wagons and carriages.

Numerous shops occupied the ground-floor levels of brick and wooden structures alike, their colourful striped awnings fluttering in the morning breeze. Clerks stood invitingly in doorways greeting passersby by name.

Shoppers were abundant. Cooks sought out freshly butchered meats and the crispest produce. Seamstresses and milliners bargained for the finest materials at lowest cost. Maids and matrons shopped for the latest fashions from Toronto, Montreal and New York.

The timeriders spotted Eliza Hammond and couldn't resist following her and two other elegantly attired women into a department store. The three women wore buttoned boots beneath their stylish skirts, shawls draped their shoulders and in their gloved hands they carried beaded handbags. Large feathered hats adorned their upswept hair.

A clerk approached immediately. "How may I help you ladies on this lovely morning?" he asked cheerfully.

"I was wondering if my order is in," said one of the women.

"I'll check on that right away, Mrs. McRobie," smiled the clerk.

"While you're back there, Clarence, will you see if the stockings from Paris have arrived?"

"Indeed, Mrs. Fairbanks," said the clerk, nodding and hastening away.

"Edna Fairbanks, Elizabeth McRobie and Eliza Hammond!" exclaimed Dilly, nudging her friend. "Can you believe?"

Laughing in amazement, the friends exited the store and continued along the boardwalk. They stopped frequently to draw each other's attention to various features.

"Look at the balconies and awnings on the upper floors," noted Azur. "They all seem to be apartments and hotels."

"If my memory serves me well, Prosper Station has seven hotels and numerous boarding houses and other lodging establishments at this time in history."

"It's a lot different seeing it for real than reading about it in books."

At Centre Street, the women stopped for a slow moving train noting the words, Michigan Central Railway, stenciled on its cars. As it proceeded south, the steam engine tooted sharp warnings of its passing.

"This must be the train that rural high school students took to school each day," said Azur.

"Take," her friend reminded her.

"Pardon?"

"You said 'took' instead of 'take'.

"Yes," laughed Azur. "It's difficult not to confuse past and present."

"Imagine Prosper Station having two railways while modern Providence Crossing has none," said Dilly.

A block further on stood the three-storied Tecumseh House. A middle-aged couple sat beneath an umbrella on the second floor balcony which ran across the hotel's frontage above the covered entrance.

"Shall we go in?" Azur asked her friend.

"I don't think I'm ready yet," replied Dilly, shivering with an unexpected and unexplained chill.

October 25

Thirteen

Rather than hang anxiously around the station as on the previous night, Azur decided that she and Dilly would remain in the security of the Isbister home until half an hour before midnight. Having her friend's company gave her a confidence she previously lacked.

When it was time to go, the timeriders steeled themselves against the probability of Faefume torment.

"It's pretty dark," said Dilly. "Where's the moon?"

"Must be obscured by cloud cover," replied Azur. "Thankfully Crescent Park rates a few street lamps."

Arm in arm, they reached the corner of Oil and Main Streets without incident. "Just one long block to go," said Azur.

"Let's try focusing on landmarks," suggested Dilly. "Where is the Isbister Inn and Bakery?"

"First we pass the Normandy Hotel and then we'll find the Inn nestled between some shops."

The women prattled on, taking comfort in the sound of their own deceptively conversational voices.

"Why, ladies, I see you're out for a late night stroll," said a low voice.

The timeriders jumped. Clutching each other's arms more tightly and looking neither left nor right, they maintained a steady walking pace.

"You needn't be afraid of me," said the voice pleasantly.

This time the women dared to glance about. There on the road, smiling at them stood a pale green figure with black shaggy hair and piercing dark eyes.

"Allow me to introduce myself," he said. "My name is Vek."

"Are you a Faefume?" asked Azur.

"I am," he said. "And contrary to what you may believe, I wish you no harm."

"Are you going to imprison us again in the spinning tunnel?" asked Dilly defiantly.

"You must have met some of my more juvenile companions," he chuckled.

"Juvenile is not the word I would use," said Dilly, taking courage from her grip on Azur's arm.

"Their way is not necessarily my way," said Vek.

"Do you have my sister?" asked Azur.

"Let me bring you to her," offered the Faefume.

"We're meeting a friend at the station," interjected Dilly.

"Chances are good that your friend won't be there," said the Faefume. "Come with me to where Hilma awaits."

Captivated by his soothing voice and intense eyes, the timeriders wavered in their intent to continue on to the station. Their indecisiveness was augmented by the effects of intoxicating vapours emanating from the Faefume.

"Leave them alone," said a commanding voice.

"They're coming with me to meet Hilma," said Vek amiably.

"Why are you here, Zhiab?" asked Azur dazedly.

"To accompany you to the depot," said the Novapetrol.

"But Hilma is waiting," she protested.

"You must trust me," said Zhiab, holding her gaze.

"Keep in mind that your train will be leaving in seven days," Vek warned the timeriders.

"Keep in mind that you want to be *on* that train," Zhiab reminded them.

"Are you coming with me?" Vek asked the women quietly.

"We have a train to meet," said Dilly, tugging on her friend's arm. "Listen to Zhiab, Az."

"What's your decision, Azur?" asked Vek.

"Not tonight," said Azur reluctantly.

"Soon then," said the Faefume, fading from sight.

Azur and Dillian proceeded to the station in the company of Zhiab.

"Why did you intervene? Azur asked him.

"To protect you," said the Novapetrol.

"But I have to find Hilma!"

"If you enter Vapourlea before you can command at least some of your powers, you will remain there with Hilma."

"How will I know when I have this…command?"

"I will tell you."

"Are you going to stick around this time and provide some training?" asked Dilly.

There was no reply. The guardian's departure was as abrupt as his arrival had been.

A distant rumbling announced the approach of the fearsome train. The timeriders waited nervously on the passenger platform as the black beast clanged into the depot and gave some final snorts and hisses before coming to a convulsive stop.

The coach door opened, steps were lowered and the conductor appeared in the doorway. Azur and Dilly held their breath.

Then to their amazement and relief, Xavier Tennyson stood in the coach doorway looking tentatively around. A sling bag dangled from one hand.

"There you are!" he called out happily when he spotted the women. In his haste to meet them, he stumbled down the iron steps as the conductor made a half-hearted attempt to steady him.

"For a neurologist he's a bit neurologically deprived," observed Azur.

"But he's so cute," said Dilly as XT hurried over to where the timeriders and the porter stood.

"Oh, XT, I'm so happy that you made it!" said Dilly.

"I see you brought additional luggage, Sir," said the porter. He set the bag from the misadventure of two days earlier at the young man's feet and returned to the station.

"Let me carry your bag," offered Azur.

A mrrrrrooooow of protest issued from the tote.

"It seems I have to be the one carrying the bag," said XT apologetically as he slipped the bag over his head and under one arm.

"You brought a cat?" asked an incredulous Azur.

"Not just any cat. Have a peek."

Azur and Dilly both drew close to look inside the tote bag. "Bleu??"

"The same," said XT. "She volunteered her escort services when I was visiting the Galvinstons. It's a long story which I will tell you later."

"A long story will definitely have to wait," agreed Azur although she was bursting to know why the family cat was here.

"Are you alright, Mister?" asked a boy unloading crates from a nearby wagon.

"Yes, thank you," replied XT. "Why do you ask?"

"You were talking to yourself," laughed his companion.

"They can't see us but they must be able to see you," said Dilly.

"Oh," said XT.

"Which means we can't take you back to the Isbisters'," said Azur.

"I'll just go to a hotel," said XT. "Can you recommend one?"

"Fletcher House is right over there," said the boy, thinking the stranger was addressing him.

"Thanks," replied XT.

"We've been planning to move to Tecumseh House," said Dilly.

"I'll go there then."

"Let's collect our belongings from Crescent Park first and then go the hotel," suggested Azur.

All seemed uneventful until the little group reached Warren Avenue.

"Oh, no!" whispered Dilly, nudging Azur to indicate three transparent green forms standing on the Isbister driveway.

"What?" asked XT, looking around and seeing nothing.

The question had barely left XT's lips when Bleu erupted from the bag and stood at his feet snarling and growling. Her greyish-blue fur stood on end, waves of violet, hyacinth, and ultramarine rippling through it. A pale blue aura surrounded man and cat.

Azur and Dilly stared with incredulity as the Faefumes disappeared, the aura faded and Bleu's coat assumed its normal state.

Taking advantage of the respite, the timeriders slipped into the house, leaving XT and Bleu outside. Then, baggage in hand, the foursome headed back to Main Street. Their route to the hotel was illuminated only by circles of light surrounding each gas lamp. Light seeped from beneath the entrances of a few saloons and hotels.

Outside one such establishment, a woman lounged in the doorway. "A handsome young stranger should not be alone," she purred. "Come inside and I'll give you a relaxing massage."

"I'm not alone," said XT.

"You look alone to me, darling," smiled the woman.

"What I mean is I'm meeting someone," stammered XT, remembering that his companions were invisible. Azur and Dilly tittered at his discomfiture.

"Keep walking," advised Dilly. "You're making it too easy for her."

As they neared Tecumseh House, a puzzling thought occurred to Azur. "How is it that you can see us?" she asked. "Do you have the mutant gene after all?"

"No but I have Bleu," he said.

Fourteen

Accompanied by the timeriders and with Bleu concealed in the sling bag, XT entered the Tecumseh House lobby. Faint light from a wall sconce near the staircase provided the only illumination. The traveller gave the call bell at the unattended reception desk a couple of taps.

Minutes passed and he was about to ding the bell again when a barefoot man still pulling on trousers over his night shirt descended the stairs.

"How d'ya get in?" he asked.

"I walked through the door," said XT.

"Shoulda been locked," grumbled the man.

"Are you the innkeeper?"

"Dennis O'Leary's the name. Me brother and me run the place."

"I need a room for a few days."

"Well you're in luck," he said sleepily. There's a room on the third floor that's unoccupied for a few days."

"I'll take it," said XT.

"Dollar fifty," said the man.

Having only the collectors coins sewn into his clothing, XT hesitated and the innkeeper thought he was resisting the lodging cost.

"Tis a fair price," he insisted. "Includes room, board and amenities for the week."

"I only have coins in large denominations," explained XT.

"In that case, we'll settle in the mornin'. Best to put your valuables in the vault. There's a lot of riffraff in the town which is why we keep the door locked. The thievery around here is shameless."

"I'll bring the coins down in the morning," said XT.

"Suit yourself. I need you to fill out the register, though, before I'll be showin' you to your room."

XT decided against an alias in case he'd entrap himself sooner or later in a web of misinformation. He wrote down that he was a physician travelling from Toronto to Detroit.

"A physician are you?" asked the innkeeper, holding a lantern in his hand as he led XT up the stairs. "We don't have a doctor lodgin' here at the time. The room you'll be takin' belongs to a salesman and his son who are off on their travels around the county."

Carrying his baggage and Bleu in her sling bag, XT followed the man up a second flight of stairs and down a long, narrow hallway. Azur and Dilly trailed close behind, carrying their own belongings. The innkeeper unlocked and entered a room on the south west corner of the hotel. His guests watched as he lit a gas lamp on a bedside table between two single beds.

"I'll be givin' you some candles in the mornin'. The sheets are fresh and there's a clean towel over there. Bathroom's down the hall, dinin' room on the main floor."

"Thank you," said XT.

"Here's the key to your room. Always lock your door. The house can't be takin' responsibility for vandalism or stolen property." With a nod of farewell, the innkeeper exited to resume his interrupted sleep.

"What an interesting view," said XT, looking out the window.

"Do you see mutants?" asked Dilly, crossing the room to see for herself. "Oh, it's eerie!"

"Mutants?" asked Azur in alarm.

"No. King Street in lamp light. There's St. Philip's Catholic Church and right behind it, St. Andrew's Presbyterian. You can even see Nemo Hall down the Street."

"Do they look the same as now?" asked Azur, peering over her friend's shoulder.

"More pristine," said Dilly. "I think it's because they're brand new."

"We should probably catch some shut eye," suggested XT.

"Guess it would've been too much to hope for three beds," said Dilly, plopping down on one of the beds. "You and I will have to share, Az. Unless you want a different bedmate."

Azur glared at her friend. "I slept on the floor in the last hotel," she said to cover her embarrassment.

"Mrroow," said Bleu emerging from her bag and stretching.

"Come here, Bleu," coaxed Azur, bending to pet the cat. Bleu accepted a brief rub before leaping onto XT's bed.

"Traitor," muttered Azur although she found it inexplicitly pleasing that her cat had adopted the young doctor. Moreover, she found it unexplainably agreeable to be sharing a room with him.

"There's no change area in this room," noted XT, pulling down the window blind. "Let me know when you want me to turn off the lamp so we can change into night attire and get some sleep."

"We had more privacy at your apartment," Dilly laughed.

"And larger cots," chuckled XT.

"Too bad you don't have any privacy here," sniffed Azur.

XT glanced over in response to the petulant comment of the young timerider. Feeling his eyes upon her, she looked up, met his gaze and mortified herself by feeling a blush spread upward from her neck into her face. The smile that flickered on the doctor's mouth annoyed her further.

"I'm engaged, remember," said Dillian mildly, unaware of the exchange between her roommates.

"Guess I can snuff the lamp now?" asked XT.

"By all means," muttered Azur.

After lying rigidly awake in the darkness scarcely daring to move lest they disturb each other, the timeriders succumbed to exhaustion and slept soundly.

In the light of early morning, XT unstitched the coins from his clothing, dressed and went down to the lobby, Bleu at his heels. The innkeeper being nowhere in sight, XT made his way to the dining room. Lodgers already breakfasting at tables covered with crisp white linens examined the newcomer with mild interest.

"Does the house have a new cat?" asked one. "Guess another mouser can never hurt," replied a different diner.

Relieved at the nonchalant response to his furry companion, XT refrained from comment and took a seat at an empty table. Bleu curled up at his feet.

"May I join you?" asked a young man entering the room and approaching XT's table.

"My pleasure," said XT.

"Name's Edward Dunn," said the man, seating himself across from the doctor and placing a napkin on his lap.

"Glad to meet you. I'm XT Barkley."

A table girl in starched apron and cap set a carafe of coffee and a pitcher of cream on the table. "I'm Loreena Dales," she said brightly to XT. "Will you be staying with us long?"

"Just a few days."

"Travelling salesman are you?"

"Doctor just passing through."

"Could we have less chitchat and more service?" snapped Edward, glaring at the waitress.

"Of course," replied the girl with a saucy curtsy. "What can I get you gentlemen to eat?"

"Bacon and eggs, please," said XT.

"With toast and marmalade?"

"Please."

"Porridge, devilled kidneys and kedigree," ordered Edward. "And don't bring the kidneys and kedigree until I'm almost finished the porridge."

"Yes, Sir, Mr. Dunn," said the girl with insolent meekness.

"What's kedigree?" asked XT after the table girl had hastened away.

"It's a lovely dish of rice, eggs and smoked fish. You've never had it?"

"Guess I knew it by another name," said XT.

"And what name would that be?" asked Dilly.

Startled, XT looked up and noticed the timeriders surveying the scene with interest and amusement. He had to suppress the urge to laugh or at the very least, comment on the unfair advantages of invisibility.

"Mr. Dunn seems to dislike the waitress," commented Azur.

"She *is* a touch brazen," noted Dilly.

"Are you here for a while?" XT asked Edward trying to tune out the distraction of a conversation that only he could hear.

"I'm a bank clerk here in town," replied Edward. "And until I find a wife, I expect I'll remain lodging at the Tecumseh."

"Surely you'll have no trouble finding a lady friend," said Loreena balancing a tray on the table edge while setting steaming covered dishes before them.

"I said *wife*, not lady friend," said Edward.

Fifteen

"What are the plans for the day?" asked XT. He, Bleu and the timeriders were in the lobby watching lodgers leave the dining room, some returning casually to their rooms, others setting off business-like for work.

"I need to discover where Hilma is being detained and, I guess, work on my powers, whatever that entails," said Azur.

"I'm going to roam through the hotel and see if I can pick up any information about my great-great's murder by eavesdropping on the staff," said Dilly.

"Do the servants in this era have the time and energy for gossiping?" asked Azur.

"No doubt there's been lots of chattering and whispering among servants in every age," said XT.

"Why don't the two of you wander around the town and leave me here," suggested Dilly.

When Azur hesitated, Dillian reminded her that it would be difficult to move through the building unobserved with XT and Bleu traipsing along in the flesh.

"Get going!" insisted Dilly. "Remember, this was the original plan, you would rescue your sister and I would solve the family mystery."

"I need spending money before I do anything," said XT, striking the call bell for service.

The innkeeper appeared at once. "What can I be doin' for you this fine mornin', Doctor?" he asked.

"I'm here to settle my bill," said XT, extracting a few coins from his pocket.

"I wouldn't be flauntin' gold and silver pieces like that publicly," cautioned the innkeeper.

"Are you able to make change?"

"I'll take me room and board, give you the balance in cash and put the other pieces in the vault if it suits you."

"That would be good, thanks," said XT, pulling a velvet pouch from his pocket and placing it on the reception desk.

"More coins?" asked the innkeeper.

XT nodded.

"My goodness, man! Why're you travellin' with all that money on you?"

"I wasn't sure how much I'd need on this trip," said XT with more honesty than the innkeeper could know.

"Here's the balance from the one gold piece," said the innkeeper, handing over a variety of coinage and a couple of bank notes. "That should hold you for a while – unless you're a gamblin' man," he added with a wink.

"Sounds fine," said XT casually.

"Wealth becomes you," observed Azur.

The innkeeper gave XT a receipt for the coins before turning to the wall of message slots and key hooks behind his desk. He swung back the far left section of slots and hooks to reveal a small vault in which he placed the coins.

Dilly waited until her friends exited the hotel and the innkeeper left the lobby. Then she sat behind the desk and flipped through the pages of the guest register. It was apparent that most of the guests were permanent, their names entered some time ago. Disappointingly, there was no listing for her great-great grandfather, Harley Witherton, even back a few years.

"Has someone been foolin' with me book?" asked the innkeeper, appearing suddenly and noticing the open register.

Dilly froze until she remembered that he couldn't see her. She slipped from the chair, tiptoed from the lobby and walked slowly through the main floor rooms. At this early hour, there was no one in the bar. In a beautifully panelled sitting room, only an elderly man sat reading near the fireplace.

At the back of the building, Dilly entered a large kitchen where the cook was preparing various casseroles. Her assistant was stirring soup that simmered in a large vat. Loreena, the table girl, stood nearby chopping vegetables and at the far end of the room, two teenage girls washed dishes.

A busty woman pushing overflowing baskets of freshly washed linens on a trolley passed through the kitchen on her way to the back courtyard. "I need one of you girls to help me hang laundry," she said to the dish washers. The younger of the girls reluctantly dried her hands on her apron and joined the laundress.

"We're running out of parsnips," Loreena told the cook. "I'll run down and get some from the root cellar."

"Hattie, you go with her and bring me some fish and wine," said the cook to her assistant.

Dilly followed Loreena and Hattie through a narrow door and down wooden steps into a large room with rough stone walls and floor. Gas lamps hanging from wall hooks cast pale light upon supplies which were stacked everywhere. Against one wall, floor to ceiling shelves were filled with canned goods and glass jars of colourful preserves.

A low doorway led to several smaller rooms, some with earthen floors and two with heavy latched doors. Hattie removed a lamp from its hook and held it while Loreena bagged parsnips from a bin in the root cellar. Then she handed over the lamp to the table girl and unlatched a heavy oak door to enter a well-stocked wine cellar where she carefully selected a half dozen bottles.

She then opened the second latched door releasing puffs of frosty air. Inside the cold room, blocks of ice sat upon racks dripping water into trays below. Slabs of pork, beef and venison hung from ceiling hooks, and ice-filled tubs contained poultry and fish.

When the servants returned to the kitchen with the requested goods, Dilly, who had spotted cabinets, chests and wardrobes in another storage room, stayed behind. The timerider carried a lantern into the dark room and set it on a dusty bureau top. Rummaging through old documents, she lost track of time until the lamp began to flicker.

"Better go upstairs before all the lamps burn out," she said aloud.

As if on cue, every lamp died out and Dilly found herself in total darkness. Moving forward cautiously, she bumped her foot against something which skittered away uttering little squeaks. Now she could hear other creatures rustling about. Fighting panic, she held her hands out to feel her way toward the stairs.

And then the light returned. Dilly gasped and turned to find the source of the sudden illumination. A greenish glow illuminated the far end of the room. Puzzled, she stared at it, hoping that a servant might put in an appearance through another of the hotel's door. But there was no servant and there didn't seem to be a door unless it was blocked by the large walnut wardrobe positioned against the glowing wall.

Dilly's skin prickled with the awareness that she was not alone.

"You know I'm here," said a low, gentle voice at her side.

"Vek?" she asked apprehensively.

"Come with me to my palace of dreams."

The seductive vapours combined with the hypnotic voice were dizzying. Dilly feared that she would faint. She tried to yell for help but could barely whisper.

"You're trembling, my dear."

"What do you want?"

"I want you."

"I'm engaged," she said feebly, her mouth barely forming the words.

"Your fiancé could never give you the endless pleasure that you'll receive from me," said the Faefume.

The timerider felt consciousness fading away.

Sixteen

On the north side of Main Street across from Tecumseh House, the striped awnings of a row of businesses fluttered in the morning breeze. Being careful to avoid bicycles and a horse-drawn carriage, Azur and XT crossed the dirt thoroughfare to get a close-up view of the wood and frame structures that comprised this section of downtown Prosper Station.

"It's amazing!" marvelled XT. "I'll never look at Providence Crossing the same way again."

"Charming as this is, I'll be happy to see Providence Crossing again."

"Do you expect to practice in Providence Crossing once you've completed your studies?"

"I hope to," she replied.

They walked in silence for a while before XT became emboldened enough to ask the reticent young woman if she had a boyfriend.

"Do you have a girlfriend?" she retorted.

"My wife died almost two years ago and I haven't been into dating," he answered.

"I'm so sorry," said Azur. "I didn't know."

"She skidded on an icy road early one January morning on her way to work and veered into oncoming traffic."

"That's terrible, XT. Are you doing okay?"

"It's getting easier. In those early months, I survived by immersing myself in my work."

"In answer to your boyfriend question, I've had a few relationships but they never lasted. All through high school, I was too young to date, and since then, I haven't met anyone that holds my interest for long. Dilly says I need to lighten up."

"Wouldn't your grandparents let you go out with boys in high school?"

Azur explained that, having started secondary school at the age of ten, she truly was too young to date. "Bram and Mavis insisted I remain there until I was fourteen although I was enrolled in university classes at the same time."

"Wow! How did that work?"

"I was able to take some courses by computer and Mavis drove me to Toronto for others. Poor dear, I've always taken her so for granted."

"Is Dilly as smart as you?"

"She's a brilliant artist, but her mother made her stay in the normal academic stream until she won a scholarship for university arts."

Absorbed in conversation as they were, XT and Azur had walked the length of town and were now back where they'd started.

"Do you smell the wonderful aroma of old fashioned yeasty bread?"

"I do," replied Azur, "but strangely, it doesn't entice me. Being a timerider is like an out-of-body experience."

"I should think so," said XT.

With Bleu at their heels, they found the source of the delicious aroma in a little grocery shop. At the shop door, a little girl with a bow atop her bouncy curls entered ahead of them holding her mother's hand. Their entry was announced by a ribbon of jangling bells tacked to the door.

A woman in her thirties came from the back to stand behind a counter near the front door. "Keep an eye on the oven, Eddie, while I attend to my customers," she called to a boy at the back.

"Doesn't Edmond have school today, Margaret?" asked the customer.

"I needed his help today because Emma is ailing," said the shopkeeper.

"Nothing serious, I hope."

"Oh no, just a bad cold."

"I'm here for some candy, please, Mrs. Rose," said the child.

"Certainly, Molly. What would you like?"

"That one and that one and that one and that one," said the child, pointing out her choices from the wooden boxes of candy displayed across the counter. She handed over a penny and the shopkeeper put the purchase in a small paper bag.

"That must be Margaret Rose!" whispered Azur. "She married when she was fourteen and had a slew of kids."

"Can I help you, young man?" asked Margaret, directing her attention to XT.

"I'd like one of those sticky buns," he replied.

"Just one? They're two for three cents," said Margaret Rose.

"Two then, please."

Out on the street once more, Azur and XT continued to stroll while XT ate one of his bakery purchases. He handed the bag containing the remaining bun to a passing boy who delightedly ran off with it down the street.

"How are you planning on finding your sister?"

"Actually, I'm starting to feel quite exasperated."

"Bleu, what are you doing out on the road?" asked XT. "You're going to get run over!"

"Mrrooow!" The cat's fur, vibrating with waves of blue and violet was standing on end.

"Does she see one of those green things?" he asked.

"I think she wants us to follow her."

XT took Azur's arm to escort her across the street. "I'm glad you're not invisible to me," he said, pleased with the blush that coloured her face.

With the humans keeping pace, Bleu raced across the street to the Tecumseh entrance.

"Dilly needs us!" said Azur, her heightened senses crying out in alarm.

Inside, they rushed up the stairs to their third floor room. Dilly was nowhere in sight.

"She said she wanted to spend time with the servants," said XT. "She can't be far."

But though they combed the building from top to bottom, they could not find her. Throughout the search, Bleu trotted along, fur bristling.

"We can hardly ask anyone if they've seen her," said XT.

"It would have to be you doing the asking since they can't see me either."

"Have you seen an invisible woman, I'd ask," joked XT, eliciting a laugh from Azur until reality intervened.

"We haven't checked the cellar," she said, worry flooding back.

As they descended the cellar stairs, her senses sent out query signals. "Evil," she said.

"Pardon?" asked XT.

"Do you feel it?" she whispered.

"The cellar is damp and musty smelling."

"It's way more than that."

There was no sign of Dilly in the first room but as they left it Bleu pushed against XT's leg and began to growl. She walked directly to the storage room and at the low doorway, sparks crackled from her now vibrantly coloured fur.

Inside, they found a dazed Dilly leaning against a brass and leather chest, and rushed anxiously to her side.

"Dilly, are you all right?" asked Azur, bending over her friend. "What happened to you?"

"Vek happened," said Zhiab flatly.

"Oh Zhiab, you're here!" said Azur looking up in relief at the beautiful mutant.

"Thoughtless, impetuous behaviour will lead to doom," he said.

"Who are you?" asked XT, eying the handsome blue figure suspiciously.

"He's Zhiab, our guardian," said Azur, pride in her voice despite the reprimand.

"Go to your room and contemplate the foolishness of wasting your remarkable gifts," said the Novapetrol. "Now!"

Back on the third floor, Dilly lay limply upon the bed she shared with Azur. In bits and pieces she described her encounter with the Faefume. "He wanted me to go with him," she said.

"Is that when Zhiab arrived?"

"I fainted and the next thing I knew, you were beside me. I didn't know Zhiab was there until he spoke to you."

"Your guardian doesn't seem overly friendly for all your fondness of him," said XT.

"We don't seem to be pleasing him," agreed Azur. "But he's infuriatingly vague! What are we doing that's thoughtless and impetuous? What gifts am I wasting?"

"We need to stick together," said Dilly, shivering. "Are you working on your powers?"

"I don't know how to do that," said Azur despairingly. "Sure, I go all tingling and electrified in the presence of danger, but what am I supposed to do then?"

"I'm going down to the dining room for lunch," said XT. "Make sure you're both here when I return."

October 26

Seventeen

Accompanied by his ever-present feline companion, XT returned from lunch to find the timeriders sound asleep, Dillian in her own bed and Azur stretched out on his. He sat down in an arm chair near the open window to read a newspaper he's picked up from the lobby. Street noises and the persistent smell of oil, scarcely noticed anymore, wafted into the room.

Azur rolled over in her sleep but the other timerider was so still that XT rose from the chair to reassure himself that she was breathing. She was, but her skin seemed to have a greenish hue. He felt for a pulse in her wrist and noted that it was appropriately slow and regular.

"Is something wrong?" asked Azur, waking.

"I don't like Dilly's colour."

Azur joined the doctor at her friend's bedside. "Dilly, are you alright?" she asked, shaking her gently.

"Mmnn."

"Dilly?"

"Yeah, I'm okay. Just tired."

"Do you remember anything at all about what happened to you in the cellar?"

"Only that I felt dizzy and lightheaded and then I felt myself slipping into oblivion."

"Did you smell anything?" asked Azur.

"Aha! I know where you're going. You think I succumbed to Vek's fumes."

"Do *you*?"

"Well, Mavis told us that Faefumes are psychic vampires."

"Is that a *yes*?"

"Maybe…"

"Remind me how that psychic vampire stuff works," said XT.

"Apparently they absorb their victim's essence while sedating them with vapours," said Azur.

"Similar to substance abuse," said XT.

"Exactly."

"Hopefully, the green skin tone will disappear once the substance leaves her system."

"Can I go back to sleep now that you've both diagnosed me?" asked Dilly, covering her face with a pillow.

As Dilly dozed off again, Azur sat on the window sill to watch the activity on the busy street below.

"Since our conversation this morning, I've been wondering how you manage to get your hospital experience," XT said to her. "Even though you flew through university courses, you need clinical hours to receive certification."

"My professors and clinical instructors have always managed to arrange blocks of clinical time for me. They seem fascinated by my insights into the healing arts."

"Insights?"

"I can often sense a person's malady just by standing nearby. My professors say I have exceptional observational skills."

"I would guess it's more than that."

"I haven't given it a lot of thought but it does seem to go beyond mere observing. Somehow I can visualize a problem area and sense blockages, temperature abnormalities and colour variations."

"Your amazing mutant gene."

"Perhaps."

"If we're going to leave Prosper Station with your sister as well as with our own hides intact, you're going to have to tap into it."

"I didn't ask you to come with us, Dr. Barkley!"

"Why are you being so testy? I'm merely pointing out that you need to acknowledge your gifts."

"Sorry," she muttered, holding back tears. "Guess I'm afraid of failing all of you."

"You won't fail us, Azur. We're on your team. Have faith in yourself."

"Now you're sounding like Zhiab."

"Maybe your guardian's telling you to work on fine tuning. You did rightly sense an evil presence in the cellar."

"But I didn't react like Bleu. Is that what you're saying?"

"I hadn't thought of that, but yes, Bleu is totally sensate."

The conversation was interrupted by firm knocking upon the door. XT cautiously opened it to find the innkeeper looking perturbed.

"Dennis," said XT.

"Sorry to be botherin' you, Dr. Barkley, but I'm deliverin' bad news."

"Oh?"

"Jackson Ewing and his son, Robert, have returned early. They're the travellin' salesmen I told you about and this be their room, I'm afraid. At the moment, they're in the pub getttin' refreshed from the journey."

"You said they'd be gone for the week."

"That I did. Seems they ran out of goods on their rounds in the county so they're back to wait for the next shipment of supplies."

"Do you have another room for me?"

"'Fraid not, Dr. Barkley, but I rang up the Johnson House and they'll fix you up right proper. I've taken care of the cost so you just have to present yourself."

"Doesn't look like I have much choice," said XT.

"So sorry."

"I'll be down within the half hour to check out and collect my items in the vault."

"You're a gentleman, Dr. Barkley, and I thank you for understandin'."

Shortly, thereafter, XT strolled eastward along the boardwalk, Bleu at his side. Also accompanying him, though unseen by most citizens of Prosper Station were the timeriders, one of whom leaned unsteadily against the other.

"We'll soon be there," XT said encouragingly. "Bleu, hop into your bag until we get to our room." The cat readily complied.

Johnson House was a large frame structure situated north of Victoria Hall and across the street from the Grand Trunk Railway and Fletcher House.

"This is where Victoria Park is now," said Azur. "John Fairbank bought the land after the hotel burned and later sold it to the town."

"Well I'm glad it hasn't burned yet because we need a place to settle into for a week," said XT.

Inside the hotel, the innkeeper awaited XT in the spacious lobby. "Welcome, Dr. Barkley," he said, extending his hand. "I'm George Johnson. If you'll be so kind as to fill out the guest register, I'll have the porter show you to your room."

The top of each register page read, 'Johnson House – Johnson Bros., Proprietors,' and beneath this it stated, 'The Proprietors will not be responsible for the loss of money, jewelry or other valuables unless deposited in the office safe. Lock and bolt your doors.'

"I will be depositing some items in your safe," said XT.

"That will be fine," said the innkeeper. "I'd like to point out that, for an additional cost, you can have a suite which might be more comfortable than a single room. Would you be interested?"

"I would," said XT. "How much do I owe you then?"

"One dollar fifty for the week. I trust you'll be satisfied."

The porter picked up the doctor's luggage and led the way down a long corridor off the lobby. They then climbed stairs to the second floor and entered a large suite overlooking Greenfield Street. XT tipped the porter and the man left with a grateful bow.

The suite had two bedrooms, each with a double bed, and a sitting room with desk and fireplace. Lounge chairs, settees and lamp tables were sprinkled throughout the rooms and floor length drapery covered the windows.

"It was worth the extra dollar fifty," Azur told XT with a smile. "Which room are you assigning us?"

"Your choice."

"You can have the green room," said Dilly. "That's not my favourite colour right now."

"Would you ladies like to browse around town or rest before dinner?" asked XT.

"Rest," replied the timeriders in unison.

"I was hoping you'd say that," said XT, removing his shoes and heading for the green room.

The timeriders detached their waist bags, set them on a luggage rack in the room papered in pale lavender flowers, and sank gratefully into a shared plump feather bed.

Although her body craved rest, Azur's mind became alert to an incoming stimulus. *Someone in the hall wants to meet me,* she thought. She tried to put the notion aside but it persisted until she gave in and rose from the bed. She opened the door and noticed an attractive young woman about her own age standing there.

"Hello," said the woman. "My name is Violet Galvinston and I saw you come in."

"Galvinston is my grandparents' name," said Azur.

"Really? I don't believe I know them."

"You wouldn't," said Azur. "How is it you can see me? Are you a mutant?"

The woman laughed. "I've been called many things but never a mutant. As for seeing you, it's very strange. My brother and I have never seen shadow people before we moved to Prosper Station."

"That's because our only stop is Prosper Station. Why do you call us shadow people?"

"You have more substance than a shadow and you're not truly transparent… but there's an unreal quality about you," said Violet. "I hope I'm not insulting you," she added.

"Not at all," laughed Azur. "Did you call me out here using telepathy?"

"I did and I knew you would come. I wanted to ask you and your friends to join my brother and me for dinner at six."

"Thank you. We'll be there."

Eighteen

Dr. XT Barkley arrived at the dining room of the Johnson House with Bleu at his feet and his timerider companions, Azur Moonstorey and Dillian Witherton, close behind. The room was formally set with starched white linen table cloths and napkins. Oil lamps surrounded by low floral arrangements graced each table. The patrons were all dressed neatly in casual dinner attire, the men wearing dinner jackets and either bow ties or Ascots with their high-collared shirts. Women wore long skirts and blouses with puffed sleeves, their figures enhanced by tight-fitting corsets.

"You've been invited to join the Galvinstons, Dr. Barkley. Please follow me," said the maître d' at the entrance. He paused to add quietly, "Bringing an animal into the dining hall is highly irregular, Sir."

"This is a rare, extremely valuable cat," said XT. "She never leaves my side."

Lips pressed in disapproval, the maître d' led them to a table beside a window through which a street lamp glowed charmingly. The table was set for five. "Will the rest of your party be joining you soon?" he enquired of the young couple seated there.

"I expect so," said Violet Galvinston. The young woman wore her tawny hair fashionably upswept, loose ringlets artfully framing her face. A circular pearl broach was pinned at the ruffled neck of her white cotton blouse with its pale pink lace decorated the wrists.

"Your waitress will be with you soon," said the maître d'. He nodded politely and returned to his post of welcome.

Violet's companion had already risen. The young man bowed to the timeriders and shook hands with XT. "Sean Galvinston," he said. "Now that we're alone for a few moments, I can acknowledge the lovely ladies," he said.

"These are my friends, Azur Moonstorey and Dillian Witherton," said XT. "It's interesting that you can see them."

"We must speak quietly of such matters," said Sean. "My sister and I have already had to flee our home and country because of our perceived differences."

Over dinner, the Galvinstons and the visitors from the future exchanged information. Violet related that she was a nurse at a small private hospital in town and Sean spoke of his accounting position with a local law firm. Originally from Salem, Massachusetts, they were sent to Canada by their father who feared for their safety. They'd been boarding at Johnson House for the past four months.

"Why did your father believe you were in danger?" asked Azur.

"Our mother was a much-loved midwife greatly in demand because of her skills and compassion. However, when one of her patients died in childbirth, she was stabbed to death by the woman's enraged husband. The man then accused her of witchcraft to save himself from hanging," said Violet.

"How terrible," said Azur.

"Why would anyone think she was a witch?" asked Dilly.

"She was an exceptional healer and prepared many of her own tinctures and ointments from herbs she grew or collected," said Sean.

"Just like my aunt and Azur's grandmother," said XT.

"Were they accused of witchcraft?" asked Violet.

"It was apparently hinted at by some," said XT.

"Does the cat belong to one of them?" asked Sean.

"Actually, she belongs to my family," laughed Azur.

"Did you say you were from Salem?" asked Dilly.

"Yes, but don't jump to conclusions. The Salem witch hunt was in the late seventeenth century, two hundred years ago," said Violet. "We're supposed to be more enlightened now."

"Nonetheless, undercurrents still exist and that why Father wanted us to have a fresh start where people didn't know us," said her brother.

"It's hard to be among strangers so far from home," said Violet, "even though Sean and I have each other here."

"My sister's getting over her loneliness," said Sean, looking at his sister with raised eyebrows.

"Don't be jealous. You'll find someone too," said Violet, taking sips of tea in a vain attempt to hide the flush that coloured her face.

"You *will* find someone," Azur assured the man who was quite possibly her great-great grandfather.

"Do you think we're related in some way?" asked Sean as if reading her thoughts.

"Well, my grandfather's name is Bram Galvinston," she said noncommittally, wishing she could share her knowledge of the future with this alienated man.

"Wouldn't it be ironic if Bram belongs to a family of sensointuitives?" asked Dilly.

"Why ironic?" asked XT.

"Because Bram gives all the credit – and blame – to Mavis," explained Azur.

"I hope sensointuitive is a complimentary term," said Sean.

"It most certainly is," said XT while Azur rolled her eyes.

The waitress came to their table to clear away dishes in preparation for dessert. "Was everything to your satisfaction?" she enquired in a lilting Irish accent. Her blue eyes rested upon the timeriders.

"You see us, don't you?" asked Azur.

The waitress nodded and departed with the tray of dishes.

"I didn't know that Mae had… special qualities," said Violet to her brother.

"Maybe she's one of those senso types," smiled Sean.

"Poor thing," Violet shared with the newcomers, "Her husband was shot not long ago at Tecumseh House. Worse yet, he was found at the scene of a murder that he's been accused of committing. Mae has no one here, and did you notice? She's pregnant."

"What's her last name?" asked Dilly.

"Witherton," said Violet. "Isn't that your last name, Dillian?" she added as an afterthought.

"Yes," said Dilly without elaborating.

"We're surrounded by coincidences," said Sean.

"Who was her husband accused of murdering?" asked Dilly.

"Julia Simpson, a writer who boarded at Tecumseh House. She was an invalid and Harley Witherton frequently delivered pharmaceuticals to her."

"Excuse me," said Dillian, rising from the table and following the waitress through the door leading to the hotel kitchen. "I'll be back shortly."

"Can I talk to you for a moment?" the timerider asked the waitress when she caught up to her.

The young woman nodded as she unloaded dishes from the tray.

"Was your husband Harley Witherton?"

Another brief nod.

"My name is Dillian Witherton and I'm interested in the circumstances surrounding Harley's murder."

"You'll be learnin' nothin'," whispered the girl.

"I'd like to clear his name."

"What do you know of my Harley and why do you care?"

"I'm probably related to him and to the babe you're carrying."

"I suppose it be possible, you having the same name and all." The waitress clattered dishes and silverware in an attempt to cover her whispered conversation.

"Did your husband like Keats?"

"He loved the poetry of Keats. How do you be knowin' this?"

"I heard that when he died he was carrying a paper that read, *When I have Fears that I may cease to be.*"

The girl wrapped her arms protectively across the skirt front of her long navy apron. "Go away," she whispered. "People will think I be daft talkin' to meself over here."

"Can we talk after work?"

The girl hesitated. Finally, she whispered, "I'll have me room to meself three nights from now. Perhaps I can be seein' you then."

"Thank you," said Dilly, wishing she could give the sad little creature a reassuring hug. Instead she left with a parting smile and joined the diners in the adjacent room.

Nineteen

"Why don't we just relax this evening and review the connections we've made so far?" suggested XT.

"Sounds good to me," said Dilly, stretching out on a brocaded chesterfield in the sitting room.

Azur sank back into a rose velvet wing chair near the fireplace and XT seated himself on the window bench seat upholstered in needlepoint.

"Interesting furnishings," commented XT.

"Beautiful," agreed Azur. "I'd enjoy it more, though, if we were carefree tourists."

"We wouldn't be here if we were tourists," said Dilly.

"Did you get a chance to speak to Mae Witherton?"

"Briefly. We're going to meet in her room three nights from now."

"What were the odds of meeting two Galvinstons and a Witherton in this hotel!" said Azur.

"Speaking of odds, imagine the significance of having two grandparents carrying the mutant gene," said XT to Azur. "You could be a super power."

"If Bram is Sean's grandson," said Azur.

"I bet he is," said Dilly. "I see a clear resemblance."

"Has your grandfather not spoken of his grandfather?" asked XT.

"Only to say he was a kind, hardworking man."

"What about photo albums?" asked Dilly. "Didn't you browse through them as a child and ask about the people in the pictures?"

"Our photo albums have a single photo of Bram's parents, one of Mavis' parents and a wedding photo of Bram and Mavis. There are a few of my mother as a baby and tons of pictures of Hilma and me."

"Why is it that we never ask questions about our family history until the knowledgeable links are gone from our lives?" wondered Dilly. "When I get back to Providence Crossing, I'm going to immerse myself in genealogy."

"When I get back to Providence Crossing, I'm going to inundate Mavis and Bram with questions," said Azur.

Bleu, who was curled up by the fireplace, languorously stretched each silvery limb, then jumped upon XT's lap. After purring contentedly for a few minutes, she moved to the window sill behind the man and stared out into the moonlit night.

"Mrrooow," she proclaimed loudly, stirring the timeriders from their drowsy musings.

"I don't see anything," said XT, rising and peering in the direction of the cat's gaze.

"Look over there," said Azur, who was now standing beside XT. "I think I see Zhiab."

"Where?" asked Dilly, jumping up to join the others at the window.

"He seems to have gone," said Azur, disappointment in her voice. "Still, I think I'll go out and look around."

"Not without us," said XT.

Accompanied by Bleu, the timeriders set out onto the streets of Prosper Station. Azur and Dilly had shawls wrapped around their shoulders against the evening chill and XT wore his jacket. Even with the waxing moon only four days short of full and regular arcs of light from the street lamps, the town was eerily dark.

An intoxicated labourer staggered from a hotel bar and wove his way unsteadily down the boardwalk. As he neared the timeriders, Bleu's fur stood on end and she began to growl. Without warning, the man bumped against XT and knocked him to the road. Tenaciously remaining at the doctor's side, Bleu surrounded them both with a protective aura of glowing purple.

The drunken man reeled towards the young women. "Why, if it isn't the pretty timeriders out for a late night of fun," he said.

"Get away from us!" said Dilly. "Look what you've done to our friend."

"I'm sure your friend can take care of himself being a physician and all."

"Who are you?" asked Azur, her skin prickling with alarm.

"Who do you think, lovely lady?" said the man brushing against her and reaching out to stroke her cheek.

As Azur shrank from his touch, she noted that his breath smelled more like gasoline than wine or whiskey. She gave him a push but he only laughed.

"Is it you, Vek?" asked Azur.

"You win the guessing prize, my dear," said the man, transforming into his lanky green form.

"Repel him with your powers, Azur!" shouted XT from the road. "I can't put weight on my leg."

"Tsk, tsk," said Vek. "Your hero seems to be disabled. He's also delusional if he thinks he can help you."

"Don't listen to him, Azur," said XT. He was now crawling along the boardwalk toward them, dragging his injured leg.

"I'm afraid my dear Azur that, if you want to see your sister, you have no choice but to listen to me."

"What do you mean?" asked Azur fighting the fear that pressed upon her.

"I mean, my dear, that only a bona fide timerider can enter the realm of the Faefumes."

"Then I'll come with her," said Dilly, linking her arm protectively into that of her friend's.

"You're more than welcome, my fiery-haired beauty," said Vek. "If you'll recall, you almost accompanied me there last night."

Dilly began to tremble at the recollection of her near escape.

"Neither of us is coming with you tonight," said Azur, putting her arm around Dilly's trembling back.

"Come, now. Afraid your powers aren't polished enough? That's a myth, you know. You don't need powers in Vapourlea."

"Leave us!" commanded Azur.

"Sorry. It's not working," laughed the Faefume breathing potent fumes into their faces.

Before Azur could will herself into a state of heightened emotion, she felt herself slipping into light-headed confusion. At the same time, she sensed Dilly slipping from her grasp and into Vek's embrace.

"Dillian," crooned the Faefume softly, "You cannot resist me."

He turned to Azur with a confident smile. "Come with us to my beautiful domain. You will be treated like princesses and have your every wish satisfied."

Seeing her friend in Vek's arms jarred Azur from her stupor. Fury erupted from the core of her being. "Let go of her, you fiend," she said in a deadly quiet voice.

Fingers rigid, she stretched out her hand and the Faefume faded away with an enraged howl. Azur stepped forward to grab Dilly before she fell, and lowered her to the boardwalk.

"Are you okay?" she asked her friend in concern.

When Dilly mumbled that she was, Azur turned her attention to XT who sat pale and perspiring nearby. "There's a broken bone in there," he said.

Azur ran her fingers gently over his lower leg and felt a bone poking jaggedly beneath the skin.

"Almost compound," XT muttered. "You'll have to splint it before you get me helped back into the hotel."

"Let me try something first," said Azur. She placed her hands gently on his calf and closed her eyes, calling for a healing power. There was no responding tingle in her body and disappointed, she opened her eyes.

Although his face was set in pain, his eyes gazed hopefully into hers. Azur experienced a surge of empathy and affection for this man who had left the safety of Providence Crossing to follow her to this terrifying place. Warmth spread from her heart, through her arms and into her hands. Her entire body felt electrified.

XT gave a grunt of pain as the bones slid back into place. He stared in wonder at his leg before taking Azur's proffered hand to rise to his feet.

"There you are, Dr. Barkley," smiled the timerider. "How do you feel?"

"Thank you, my angel nurse," he whispered, hugging Azur tightly. "You have an amazing gift!"

"It's not Victorian to hug in public," said Azur, extracting herself from XT's embrace. "We better get Dilly back to bed."

October 27

Twenty

Azur lay awake long after Dilly had drifted into a restless sleep. She wondered if XT was awake in the adjacent bedroom and sensed that he was.

He really does like me, she thought, reliving the rush of pleasure his grateful hug on the boardwalk had stirred in her. Of course, he would be grateful for having a broken leg repaired, she reminded herself. He's probably still grieving for his wife and I'm nothing more to him than a means of accessing his research on hypersensory abilities and auras.

When morning finally came, XT went down to breakfast with his ever-present feline companion. Azur and Dilly, having no need for food, remained in bed.

Unable to sleep, Azur soon rose, dressed and went into the sitting room. When XT returned, he found her at the window seat absently surveying the comings and goings of people and animals on the streets below.

"Five nights from tonight we have to board the train," announced XT when he returned from the dining room.

"Do you think I don't know that?" asked Azur.

"Sorry. I wasn't trying to alarm you. Just wondering how you wanted to spend your day."

"I'm restless so I'm going out for some exercise. I'll do some more town touring and people watching. Maybe I'll happen upon some telling interactions. It all seems to be a matter of luck."

"You've been pretty lucky so far," said XT.

"I'm no closer to finding Hilma," she sighed.

"I think you are. You've established relationships with assorted mutants, including human types, and you're getting a feel for the old town."

"Do you want to come with us?"

"Certainly. I have no intention of letting you out of my sight," said XT.

"Let's read for an hour and let Dilly sleep. By that time, the stores will all be open and people will be shopping and attending to business."

Already the sounds of commerce floated upward through the autumn air. While XT perused his newspaper, Azur listened to the nearby sounds of swishing bicycle tires, clomping hooves and clattering service wagons upon the dirt road. Voices rose and fell exchanging morning greetings and discussing business.

When XT finished his paper, he rose and stretched. "We should check on Dilly," he said.

Dilly opened her eyes when her friends entered her lavender sanctuary. "Do you mind if I spend the day in bed?" she asked, snuggling under the covers. "Perhaps I'll sleep better in daylight when I'm less likely to dream of green vampires stealing my soul."

"As long as you stay here and don't go prowling around cellars," said Azur.

"No danger of that," said Dilly. "I'm too exhausted."

Shortly thereafter, XT, Azur and Bleu stood on the corner of Greenfield and Main observing the busy street scene. Kiddy corner from them, at Grand Trunk Station, a train was taking on freight and passengers. Railway workers milled about carrying out their routine tasks. Horses hauling wagons heaped with oil drums were already queuing up near the platform.

"Shall we visit the station?" asked XT offering his crooked arm to assist her across the street.

As they stepped off the boardwalk, a horse and carriage trotted quickly around the corner. XT pulled Azur close to shield her from the dirt kicked up by the horses' flying hooves. She felt a delicious tingle where the pressure of his hand touched her arm.

"Do you feel as if we've known each other longer than a week?" she asked him, averting her eyes as shyness bewildered her.

"I'd be afraid to admit it," he said. "You've already accused me of being a stalker."

"That was before I knew you."

"And now you do?"

"Not really," she mumbled, feeling naïve and annoyed at the same time.

"You're a fascinating young woman," said XT.

"You're an intriguing older man, Dr. Barkley."

"I can't be more than six or seven years older than you," he said defensively. "Of course, I am a stalker."

She laughed, and the tension between them eased.

"I shouldn't tease you," he said, giving her shoulder a squeeze. Then he took her hand and led her safely across the street to the boardwalk on the northwest corner of Main.

"We're not going to the station?" she asked, covering her disappointment that he had released her hand as soon as their boots left the roadway.

"I think we should come back when it's less chaotic," he said.

They walked slowly along the boardwalk, Bleu keeping pace at XT's feet.

"What are you thinking?" he asked her after several minutes of silence.

"I'm in turmoil," she admitted. "Time is running out to make contact with Vek and allow him to take me to my sister.

I'm impatient to get this over with and terrified that I might remain in Vapourlea forever."

Absorbed in worrisome thoughts and lacking a better way to fill the morning hours, they continued walking until they found themselves at the entrance of Margaret Rose's shop. Inside the store, Mrs. Rose was arranging candy sticks in glass jars along the counter top.

She looked up and smiled when she saw XT. "You've come back for my famous sticky buns," she said.

"Couldn't resist," he said, although that had not been his intent.

"Two again?" she asked.

"Just one today."

As Margaret Rose bent over to retrieve a freshly baked bun, the floor seemed to shift beneath the timeriders' feet. Azur grabbed XT's arm to steady herself. Bleu growled and positioned herself against XT's legs. The candy counter with its scented bakery display disappeared before their startled eyes, replaced by wooden bins of root vegetables, cabbages and apples. Shelves along one wall were stocked with canned goods and assorted grocery supplies and at the back of the store, a dark-haired man cheerfully popped corn in a large kettle atop an iron wood stove.

A young boy in short pants and knee socks ran into the store, attracted by the aroma of the fresh popcorn. His mother hurried in behind him, frowning in disapproval.

"Bloss, it's much too early in the day for popcorn," she reprimanded the boy.

"Please, Mother!" begged the boy. "Mr. Isber wouldn't be making it if it was too early."

"He's preparing it for later," scolded the woman.

"Good morning Mrs. Sutherland," said Lotto Isber. "Haven't seen you in a while."

"I don't come to Prosper Station often but Bloss and I accompanied Mr. Sutherland today. He needed to pick up something at VanTuyl and Fairbank Hardware."

"I suppose you usually shop in Oil Centre."

"Usually," she admitted. "Unless I'm looking for fashion items at the department stores in this town."

"*Please*, Mother," said Bloss, tugging at his mother's skirt.

"There you are, Peggy," said a man entering the store.

"Bloss ran in here for popcorn," explained the woman to her husband.

"Put some in a bag for him, Lotto," the man instructed the grocer. "The young rascal can have it later."

"You do spoil him," said Peggy Sutherland.

Azur and XT watched the transaction in puzzlement and concern.

"This can't be good," said Azur. "Lotto Isber didn't sell vegetables at this location until the early twentieth century. We seem to have slipped ahead about ten years."

"That's because your doctor friend is interfering with our plans to reunite you and your sister," said a thin man leaning against a potato bin. "You should really part from his company."

Nattily attired in dark grey waistcoat and top hat, he glared at XT with threatening dark eyes. Growling and yowling, Bleu stood between XT and the stranger, wild blue hair rippling with mauve and violet.

Before Azur and XT could fully react, the man in grey was pulled to his feet by a tall man wearing a long navy overcoat. While the timeriders watched in amazement, the shape shifters morphed into the more recognizable forms of Faefume and Novapetrol, Vek and Zhiab.

Throwing back his head in defiant laughter, Vek faded away.

Zhiab turned to Azur. "You must liberate all your powers soon, young Senso" he said. "The full moon will adorn the sky three nights hence."

"Zhiab, wait," said Azur. But the guardian, like his green nemesis, had disappeared.

"Here's your sticky bun, Sir," said Margaret Rose, holding out a paper bag to XT.

"One cent for one bun," XT prompted himself aloud, reaching into his pocket while struggling to comprehend the fluctuating events of the last hour. Or had it been mere minutes?

Mrs. Rose accepted the coin from his outstretched hand before rushing off to the back of her shop to remove a rack of baked goods from the oven and to discipline one of her boisterous brood.

Twenty-one

No sooner had Azur and XT left the suite, then there was a discreet tap on the door and a chambermaid entered to tidy up the room and remove waste.

"Sorry, Miss," she said as she poked her head into the room where Dilly lay half asleep. "I didn't know there was anyone here. Shall I leave and come back later?"

"Will you be long?" mumbled Dilly.

"I can empty the waste and leave it at that, if you so wish, Miss."

"Go ahead then, please."

As Dilly listened sleepily to the chambermaid moving from room to room, it occurred to her that she was not invisible to the girl. "You can see me," she said when the maid returned to the room where the timerider lay abed.

"Yes, Miss. We don't get shadow people here often, and then, always before Hallowe'en."

"Are there many like you with the giftedness?"

"Giftedness?" The girl laughed, savouring the word. "If folks knew about us, they'd send us away. In answer to your question, there are very few of us. It seems to run in families."

After the maid left, Dilly rolled over with a sigh to resume sleeping. Minutes later she thought she heard further tapping. "Go away," she murmured into her pillow. "I'm not getting up to answer the door."

"Excuse me, Miss," said the chambermaid from the doorway of Dilly's room. "I finished your suite and was still up here working."

"Yes?" Dilly wondered why the girl was giving her an update on her work progress.

"Well, there's a visitor outside wanting to see you for a minute. Can I show her in?"

"A visitor?" Dilly asked in alarm.

"It's the dining room girl, Mae Witherton, but I can tell her you don't wish to be disturbed, Miss."

"No, no! Please send her in."

Mae Witherton approached Dilly's bed and stood there wringing her hands. "One of the other table girls be coverin' for me," she explained, "so I can stay but a few minutes."

"I'm happy you came," said Dilly, sitting up in bed and pushing strands of hair from her face.

"Are you unwell?" asked Mae.

"I've had a couple of sleepless nights," said Dilly.

"I got to wonderin' how you knew about the paper my Harley had on him when he died and I couldn't wait two more nights to talk with you."

"It's family history," said Dilly, wondering how she could explain twenty-first century knowledge to a young woman living in the late nineteenth century.

"How can it be family history when he's been dead but a few weeks?" asked Mae. "Does this have something to do with you being a shadow person?"

"It does," said Dillian. "Forget that I used the word, *history*. But I do believe it's common knowledge."

"Common knowledge that my Harley be a murderer," said Mae bitterly. "He was a gentleman and kind to everyone he met."

"Come and sit down," said Dilly, indicating an armchair near the bed. "You should keep off your feet whenever you can."

Mae Witherton sat down with a sigh. She was pale and looked exhausted.

"What happened the night your husband died?"

"I only know what the police told me and I don't believe any of it."

"Tell me everything you know and I'll try to help you."

"Would you like to see the poem?" Mae Witherton removed a folded paper from her apron pocket and handed it to Dilly who accepted it with reverence. The paper was worn from frequent handling especially along the creases where it had been folded. There were smears of dried blood on it, faded now to brown. The words were hand written in elegant penmanship.

When I have Fears that I may cease to be

When I have fears that I may cease to be
before my pen has glean'd my teeming brain,
before high-piled books, in charact'ry,
hold like rich garners the full-ripen'd grain;

When I behold, upon the night's starr'd face,
huge cloudy symbols of a high romance,
and feel that I may never live to trace
their shadows, with the magic hand of chance;

And when I feel, fair creature of an hour!
that I shall never look upon thee more,
never have relish in the faery power
of unreflecting love! - then on the shore
of the wide world I stand alone, and think
till love and fame to nothingness do sink.

John Keats 1795-1821

"I love Keats," said Dilly, looking up from the paper.

"So did Harley," said Mae. "He used to read to me whenever we both weren't workin'. He would also read to Julia Simpson whenever he brought her tonic to Tecumseh House and she would share her writin' with him. The police tried to make something bad out of it, but they're wrong."

"Is Julia Simpson the woman who died?"

"Yes. Someone stabbed Julia to death but it wasn't my Harley."

"Do you know who did?"

"No," said Mae, shaking her head in distress.

"Do you think it was Harley who brought the Keats sonnet to Julia?"

"I know he did. I watched him copy it out by hand the night before he took it to her. He wouldn't come to bed until he was finished."

"Do you know why he took it to her?"

"The police said it be proof he loved her which is untrue! Harley told me Julia wanted a copy because she felt she and John Keats had a lot in common."

"Oh?"

"You see, they both were invalids with consumption and they both were writers. Julia had spent the previous winter in California with her sister and she thought she was cured. But she worsened terribly after she returned to Tecumseh House. She told Harley that Keats died when he was twenty-six years old and she would not be seein' that age herself."

"I imagine she meant death by consumption, though, and not by stabbing," said Dilly.

"To be sure."

"Was there a witness to the stabbing?"

"Two witnesses so the police said. Loreena Dales and Edward Dunn."

"What do the police say happened?"

"They said Edward Dunn heard a commotion in Julia Simpson's room and found Harley standin' there with a bloody knife. Loreena and Julia were covered with blood and Harley was rantin' like a mad man. So Edward Dunn ran back to his room, got his gun and shot my Harley. The police said it was fortunate Harley died and spared me the humiliation of a trial and worse."

"I think it was Loreena who served XT his breakfast at Tecumseh House yesterday," said Dilly. "Had she been stabbed too?"

"No. It was all Julia's blood. The police told me Loreena had been tryin' to save Julia."

"What did the police say was the motive for the killing?"

"They said Harley was a spurned lover. Of course I'm not believin' it. My gentle Harley had the greatest respect for Julia Simpson."

"Were Loreena Dales and Edward Dunn friends of Julia?"

"Quite probably. They all lived in the same hotel. Loreena bein' a table girl would have brought meals to Julia's room. And Edward is a bank clerk who boards at Tecumseh House down the hall from where Julia lived."

"I believe you said that Harley brought tonic to Julia on a regular basis."

"Yes he was an apprentice to the druggist who had him drop it off on his way home from work in the evenin'."

"Do you know what was in the tonic?"

"It was laudanum to help the cough and the pain, my Harley told me. Miss Simpson was usin' a lot of it toward the end."

"Would anyone kill for laudanum?"

"Why would they, it bein' a common remedy anyone can purchase at a pharmacy even for colicky babies?"

Not in my time, thought Dilly. *Opium added to wine is rather frowned upon.* Aloud she asked, "Did you mind Harley coming home late in the evenings?"

"My evenin's were later than his. Harley was always in our room waitin' for me by the time I finished up in the dinin' room. He felt bad that I worked such long hours. He would have tea ready for me and insist that I put my feet up." Mae Witherton began to cry softly.

"It sounds like you and Harley were very much in love," said Dilly. "How did you meet?"

"He was lodgin' here at Johnson House when I started in the dinin' room four years ago. I was fifteen and he was twenty-one. He was so smart and handsome with his red hair and all. Darker than yours it was and he liked to tease me whenever he came for meals and I was waitin' tables." Mae smiled sadly at the memory.

"And then you got married," said Dilly.

"A year ago," she nodded. "It was so nice to move from the servants' quarters to his room like a regular lodger. We wanted to save enough for a little house before there be a baby – but things don't always go as planned."

"It's nice you're going to have Harley's baby," said Dilly.

"Yes," smiled Mae. "Harley surprised me by bein' happy when I told him my suspicions. He told me not to worry, that we'd be fine."

"Will you stay here once the baby's born?"

"They won't let me work here unless I give up my wee one."

"Surely you wouldn't do that!"

"I still have most of a month to be workin' things out."

"What kind of arrangements do you need?"

"It would be nice to find a rich family that be lookin' for a governess and who would let me raise my child with theirs. Do you think I be dreamin'?"

"Follow your dreams, Mae," said Dillian, adding silently, *because you are most likely carrying my great-grandfather.*

Twenty-two

"There's the water wagon making rounds," said XT that afternoon. "And look! An ice wagon is pulling in right behind it."

Azur joined him at the hotel's sitting room window. Below them a team of two white horses was hitched to a wagon bearing a large wooden drum of water which had been laboriously hauled from the St. Clair River thirty-eight kilometers away at Port Sarnia. The second wagon, pulled by two brown horses, was filled with blocks of ice buried in sawdust. The ice was cut from frozen Lake Huron in winter and stored in ice houses for the rest of the year.

"I'm going to go down and chat with those drivers," said XT. "Then I'd like to follow the boardwalk down to Bridgeview Park before supper. Do you want to come?"

"I don't think so," said Azur. "I may go and chat with the Galvinstons. Anyway, with all the working oil wells down there, you'd be the only one in Prosper Station to consider it a park."

"The Flats then," laughed XT. "Along the way, I might take a look at the Gillespie Mansion and then stop off to see how the Fairbank place is coming along."

"Will you be having tea then at Sunnyside?" asked Azur with playful pomposity.

"I'm sure Edna Fairbank *would* extend a personal invitation to me but I don't believe she's moved in yet."

"Oh, I forgot. The mansion's not quite built."

The timeriders exchanged amused glances before XT left on his historical outing. Azur checked on Dilly and told her she was going to see if the Galvinstons were in.

"Your colour's improving," she assured her friend.

"I'm starting to feel better," said Dilly. "This evening I'll go out with you and XT and get some fresh air."

"You must be feeling good about your conversation with Mae."

"I am," said Dilly. "And now that I know her personally, I'm more determined than ever to solve Harley Witherton's murder."

Leaving her friend in bed, Azur set off in search of the Galvinstons. Neither Violet nor Sean was in their suite or in any of the hotel lounges. Johnson House was quiet in the autumn afternoon, the lodgers apparently out or resting. At that time of day, most of the activity was in the laundry and kitchen areas.

Azur went outside to wander the gardens which, although they had been mulched in preparation for the winter, still flaunted bursts of autumnal colour. She recognized golden chrysanthemums, mauve eupatorium, rose sedum and delicate asters in shades of pink, purple and white. Next door to the hotel, Victoria Hall, as beautiful and stately as in modern Providence Crossing, stood proudly in the afternoon sunshine. *I love this town*, Azur thought, momentarily forgetting her grim mission.

She returned to the hotel through a back door and was attracted by the sound of voices and laughter coming through a door off the summer kitchen. Curious, Azur followed the sound down a flight of stairs into an open storage area full of supplies and storage bins. In the illumination cast by gas lamps hanging from wall hooks, Azur detected motion behind a row of boxes and trunks. A young man and a kitchen maid, clothes in disarray, were exchanging heated kisses and caresses.

Azur was about to return upstairs when she heard her name called softly. She looked about and saw Zhiab leaning against the stone cellar wall. She couldn't help but admire how striking he looked with his dark shoulder-length hair, blue complexion, prominent cheek bones and almond-shaped eyes.

"Zhiab!" she exclaimed.

He smiled warmly and beckoned for her to approach. She happily obliged and when she drew near, he reached out to her and pulled her close. "My lovely Azur," he said in a low, quiet voice.

Initially surprised, the timerider allowed herself to nestle against him, surrendering to his intoxicating presence. She felt herself drifting, falling, floating, delirious. He put his hand under her chin, tilting her face upward and she closed her eyes, anticipating the pressure of his lips upon hers. Instead he pushed her gently away.

"Later," he said softly.

"Yes," she agreed, chastened. "I must not be distracted from the search for my sister."

"No need to delay further. I will take you there now." He took her hand and led her to a small doorway a few feet away which, strangely, she had not noticed before and which now widened into the mouth of a cavern.

Belatedly, Azur felt unmistakable warning twinges of grave danger and sensed the essence of evil. She wondered why she had failed until now to detect the heady aroma of petroleum fumes surrounding her. When she tried to remove her hand from his, he grasped it more determinedly and dragged her toward the cave.

Bewildered, she raised her head to observe the attractive Novapetrol features shifting from blue to green while melting into a grinning Faefume face with glittery round eyes and short shaggy hair.

"Vek," she whispered in horror.

"Come with me to my palace of dreams."

The hypnotic voice and seductive vapours were dizzying. Azur recalled Dilly relating her own similar experience with the Faefume.

"Zhiab!" she tried to call out, but no sound came from her lips.

Suddenly the vampire released his grip on her and sailed backward into the cave. His face registered shock before the wall closed over, sealing him from view.

"Impetuous behaviour leads to doom," said the guardian. "You are not yet ready to enter Vapourlea."

"Zhiab, is it really you?" she cried, throwing her arms around him. Still under the influence of the toxic vapours, she pressed against him, breathing in his wonderful scent of forest freshness and shivered with delight.

"Hold me," she whispered.

The guardian placed his hands firmly on her upper arms and shook her roughly. "How could you let your guard down so badly?" he asked. "You know you cannot trust Vek, that he is deceitful and will lead you astray."

"I thought you liked me," she said, stung by his rejection.

"I love you," he said.

Gazing up at his tranquil face, Azur knew that the guardian's love was genuine and pure.

"Return to your room," he said and was gone.

Unaware of the drama that had taken place nearby, the servant lovers emerged from behind the chests and boxes, rearranged their clothes, brushed by Azur and ran tittering up the stairs.

Back in their suite, Azur sat beside Dilly on the edge of the bed. "Why did I behave so shamelessly?" she cried.

"Vek is extremely seductive," sympathized her friend.

"It's not just Vek. I made a fool of myself with Zhiab."

"No you didn't, Az. Zhiab told you he loved you. It seems your affection is reciprocal."

"I was so easily swayed. Am I that fickle?"

"It was an exceptional situation," Dilly reassured her.

"I've been here six days and I've made no contact with Hilma. Meanwhile, I'm running about throwing myself at mutants, one of them a vampire."

"*Psychic* vampire," said Dilly.

"I'd rather have the bite marks. It's less insidious."

"XT will soon be back from his walk, my energy is finally returning and you, Azur Moonstorey, will soon regain your equanimity. This evening we'll combine our wits and proceed on our mission with confidence!"

"Dil, you're an angel."

"Angels come in different forms," she smiled.

"Were you thinking of Zhiab?"

"For sure. But you also have a certain doctor who would do anything for you."

"XT is very nice…"

"Do I hear a *but*?"

"Compared to Zhiab, he's rather…"

"Human?"

October 28

Twenty-three

At breakfast the next morning, XT regaled his table with descriptions of his tour of the flats. He admitted that he didn't linger long because he was not dressed to wander through the oil-drenched mud. "It was a bee hive of activity around those wells," he said. "Men digging and drilling, horses pulling huge barrels of crude…"

"I understand you also stopped by the Fairbank mansion," said Sean. "How's it coming along?"

"They're well into bricking it now," said XT. "The labourers were telling me that the wood used for construction came from the Fairbank farms and the bricks were shipped from Ohio individually wrapped in wax paper."

"So I've heard," said Sean. "Apparently it's going to have twenty-two rooms including a ball room on the third floor."

Before Violet excused herself from the table, she invited the timeriders to stop by the private hospital where she worked, Azur and XT were eager to see nineteenth century medicine firsthand. Dilly, however, begged off, saying she would remain in the main lounge of Johnson House reading.

"You're not playing matchmaker sending the two of us off together?" Azur asked her friend suspiciously.

"I'm repelled by blood and gore," replied Dilly. "I'm an artist, remember?"

The hospital was a lovely Ontario Cottage with a filigreed verandah, multipane windows, an upper dormer and wrought iron cresting atop its hip roof. Situated on Main Street west of the business section, it was owned by Dr. George Lougheed who lived there with his wife, Vanda.

A patient, his face a mask of thickly-dabbed aluminum paste, sat on the verandah in one of four wicker lounge chairs. He nodded to XT as he and the invisible timerider made their way to the front door. In response to doorbell chimes, a nurse ushered XT into a narrow hall where outpatients on straight back chairs awaited their turns with the doctor.

Dr. Lougheed emerged from the first door on the left. "Miss Galvinston told me to expect you, Dr. Barkley," he said, shaking hands with his visitor.

"It's kind of you to make time for me, Dr. Lougheed," said XT.

"Happy to oblige. I'm sure your facilities in the city are much grander than my humble one."

"The personal touch is the most important factor in the healing arts," said XT.

"Quite so! Well, this is my surgery," he said, leading XT into a room with an examining table, two chairs, a desk and several glass-fronted cupboards stocked with medical instruments, bottles and vials.

"You don't mind me showing the doctor around?" asked Dr. Lougheed of a woman lying on the table beneath a cotton sheet. "I'll be back momentarily."

"No, Doctor," she said meekly.

"Mrs. Fowler is expecting her third child in four years," he said as he exited the surgery. "Good producer she is."

Accompanied by the invisible Azur, XT followed the doctor from the room.

"When the missus and I moved in, that was a parlour in there," he said, pointing at double French doors off the east hall wall. "Now it's a three-bed ward. This room behind the surgery is our bedroom. It leads to an upstairs sitting room with a dormer window."

George Lougheed led the way into a long rectangular room that ran the width of the house separating the front section from the bathroom, kitchen, pantry and laundry facilities. The room was divided into three sections by large square pillars and valences, and like the hall, had oak flooring and wainscoting.

The westernmost end of the long room was graced with a wide stone fireplace which had glass-fronted bookcases built in on either side. The eastern section of the room which served as the hospital's supply room had a second fireplace against the north wall and a charming window seat under an east bay window.

The middle, and largest of the three sections, contained five beds some concealed behind privacy screens. Each bed was meticulously made up with ironed white sheets, pillow cases and spread. A coarse woolen blanket was fan-folded across the bottom.

"I try to keep up on the latest medical practices and information," said Dr. Lougheed.

"Your place is beautiful," said XT sincerely. "Prosper Station is fortunate to have you."

"There are four physicians here actually."

"You must rate at the top," said XT.

Dr. Lougheed smiled appreciatively. "I'm going to leave you with Miss Galvinston while I get back to my patients. I have a busy day ahead."

XT thanked him and went with Azur to find Violet. They located her in the parlour ward, bathing a patient behind a privacy screen.

"Be with you in a minute," she said. When she was able to join her visitors, she took them on a brief walk-about of the patients beginning in the five-bed ward.

"Rounds," said Azur.

"Like at a teaching hospital," smiled Violet. "Do you do that where you come from?"

"Yes," said XT. "Though not all patients appreciate how it's really to their advantage to have several minds pondering their conditions."

"We don't have rounds here but our patients *are* accustomed to the Ladies Auxiliary popping in from time to time with bandages and treats."

"How many people work here" Azur asked.

"Let's see," said Violet. "There are three nurses during the day and one at night. Then there's a kitchen girl, a char woman and a gardener who doubles as maintenance man. Mrs. Lougheed manages the place. So we probably have a staff of more than a dozen."

The timeriders followed Violet to the first bed. "This is Mr. Jeffs, a brakeman who lost his lower limbs in a train collision. He's been with us several weeks."

"How are you doing, Mr. Jeffs?" inquired XT.

"I'll be off dancin' on me wooden legs as soon as the carpenter has me fitted up," he said jovially.

"Good luck to you," said XT.

"Here's Mr. Rawlins. He's doing quite well."

"What is your ailment, Mr. Rawlins?" inquired the visiting physician.

"Well, young fella, I'm not certain that smuggling opium across the border is an ailment."

"You were caught?"

"And brought back to our lovely local gaol. Seems the police later found me unconscious in my cell and brought me to this fine hospital to have my stomach pumped. Unpleasant business."

"You swallowed some of your opium, I take it," said XT.

"Yes. Those damnable gut bags burst before completing their journey."

"Fortunate you are that they didn't burst in your intestines," said Violet.

"Then I'd be dead like my brother," he agreed. "It was a railway accident took him just last year.

"I'm sorry," said XT.

Rawlins shrugged. "Well, life is for the living, they say."

XT nodded.

"In a couple of hours the police are coming to take me back to the opera house."

"The opera house?" asked the doctor.

"I have a lovely little cell in the basement of Victoria Hall where I'll most likely have a different drunk every night for company until my trial."

"Don't speak ill of the intoxicated," said the patient in the next bed.

"Mr. Smithers came to us with several gashes on his face and arms," said Violet, moving to the next bed. "As you can see, he was in a bit of a fight."

"Our lovely nurse is being discreet," said Smithers. "Put more plainly, I was brawling at one of our local pubs."

"What's your occupation, Mr. Smithers?" asked XT.

"I'm an undertaker and when I'm not embalming a corpse, I'm pickling myself." He laughed at his own hilarity.

The fourth bed was occupied by a sleeping boy recovering from an appendectomy.

Violet explained that the empty fifth bed belonged to the patient they had passed on the verandah. "Mr. Graham is a railway brakeman who was scalded on the face and arms."

"Do you get many burn patients?" asked Azur.

"All the time. Just last week we admitted an oil worker burnt in a nitroglycerin explosion. He didn't survive long, poor soul."

They proceeded into the parlour ward where in the first bed, a woman sat propped up on pillows reading.

"I can hardly turn the pages," she said, indicating her bandaged hands.

"Severe poison ivy reaction," said Violet.

"Can you imagine!" said the woman, "And me with so much work awaiting at home."

"Your family will manage somehow, Mrs. Burrows," said Violet. "Enjoy the rest you're getting."

Mrs. Burrows shook her head woefully.

Azur and XT then followed Violet over to the window bed where behind a privacy screen, an emaciated woman lay curled on her side, eyes closed, complexion a sickly grey. "Nurse, can I have more medicine?" she asked in a barely audible voice.

"I'll bring you some shortly," promised Violet. Azur laid her hand gently on the suffering form and the woman relaxed visibly.

"Cancer of the stomach," Violet said quietly to the visitors as they crossed to the third bed which was positioned against the draped French doors.

"This young man was brought in last evening by my fiancé, Barrington Creswell," she said. "Daniel Racher is a stable boy at Fletcher House where Barrington's lodging until he builds his own place."

"Your fiancé brought him here?" asked Azur.

"I'll tell you about Barrington sometime," whispered Violet.

"Hello, Daniel," said XT to the patient. "What happened to you?"

"I was kicked by a horse while I was cleaning out a stall and I fell against a wall hook. Cut my arm."

"Quite a gash he had," said Violet. "It needed twenty stitches and since Daniel also has abdominal bruising, Dr. Lougheed is keeping him under observation."

"Nurse, can you get a message to Charlene Murray for me?" asked Daniel. "We were supposed to meet up last night and she'll be wondering where I am."

"I'll see what I can do," said Violet. "Is Charlene your girlfriend?"

"Yes but we haven't told anyone."

"Ask him if Charlene works for the Isbisters," said Azur.

"That's part of the problem," replied Daniel to the nurse's repetition of Azur's question. "She'd lose her job if the Isbisters found out she had a boyfriend."

"Servants can't have boyfriends?" asked Azur.

"Servant relationships are discouraged," said Violet, answering Azur cleverly while giving Daniel the impression she was responding to him. "People don't want the young ones to marry although widows and older servants whose children are grown are okay."

"They like their servants at their beck and call day and night," noted XT.

"And pregnancies and young children would interfere," added Azur.

"Precisely," said Violet, nodding at XT and making eye contact with Azur.

"It's even worse than that," said Daniel.

"How is it worse?" asked Violet.

"Charlene and I were going to elope last night because I have to leave town."

"Why do you have to leave town?" asked Violet.

"I witnessed a murder," he whispered.

Twenty-four

Azur, Dilly, XT and Bleu walked to the Isbister house in mid-afternoon to deliver Daniel Racher's note to Charlene Murray. The servant girl came to the front door in response to XT's knocking.

"My name is Dr. Barkley," said XT. "Are you Charlene Murray?"

"I am," she replied cautiously.

"I have a note for you from Daniel Racher."

"A note from Daniel? Is he alright? Where is he?"

"Don't worry, he's fine, but he's in Dr. Lougheed's care."

"Better come inside so that no one hears me talking about Daniel," she said, admitting him to the enclosed entranceway. "Sir, please leave the cat outside."

Bleu's fur stood on end. "Mrrooow!" she said loudly.

"Is something wild about to happen?" XT asked the timeriders who, unseen by the servant, had squeezed into the enclosed space with him.

"No, Bleu's still annoyed that you didn't take her to Violet's hospital," said Azur. "She's not about to get separated from you again."

"It's a valuable cat and I can't leave her alone," XT told Charlene.

"I've never heard of such a thing!" clucked the servant girl. "Well let it in then."

"It's a bit crowded in here," muttered Dilly, pressed against the stain glass in the small outer entrance. "Isn't she going to at least let us into the front hall?"

"I'd invite you inside, Sir, but those little boys have big ears and I don't want them passing on information about me and Daniel."

"Ask her who's playing the piano," said Azur.

"Is that one of the boys playing the piano?" asked XT to humour Azur.

"No, that's Alice home from school with a bad cold. She was pestering me so I told her to do some practicing and then I'd give her some cookies and milk."

"Bribery works in every era," noted Dilly.

"Tell me about Daniel. I'm about to burst with worrying."

"I think he explains it in this note," said XT, passing Charlene a folded paper retrieved from his coat pocket. "He told me to wait for your reply.

The girl reached for the note anxiously and read it over several times. "It doesn't say much," she said, disappointment in her voice. "Just that he'll be in the hospital for a few days and that he'll see me after that. Do you know about me and Daniel?"

"Daniel told me about your plans to elope," said XT. "Do you think that's wise?"

"Daniel says he could be in serious trouble for witnessing those killings at Tecumseh House. I won't let him leave town without me."

"Tell her not to be hasty," said Azur. "If Daniel can help us solve the case, they won't have to go anywhere."

"There are some new developments in that situation," said XT. "Daniel may not be in any danger."

"That still wouldn't help me," said Charlene. "Daniel and I want to get married and I know my father won't hear tell of it."

"Her father probably thinks she's too young," said Dilly.

"Does he think you're too young?" asked XT.

"I'm fifteen but lots of girls get married at that age."

"I would think that *some* girls must wait until they're older," said XT.

"Well yes, the ones who are rich and go on to school. Or the ones who stay on as servants until they're too old and wizzled up for any man to look at."

"How old is Daniel?"

"Nineteen."

"Both you and Daniel have jobs in this town," said XT. "How would you make a living if you left Prosper Station?"

"Daniel says we'd find a farm that would take us both on."

"Do you have one in mind?"

"No, but I expect there are lots of them out there."

"Tell her they mightn't be treated as well as they are now," said Azur.

XT complied, adding, "Do you and Daniel like your employers?"

"Daniel's been working at the Fletcher Livery & Stables since he was thirteen. He's the senior stable boy now and Mr. Fletcher sometimes lets him drive the carriages."

"It sounds like he has a decent job."

"I guess."

"What about you?"

"It's not as cheerful here as it was when Mr. Isbister was alive. Everybody goes around all solemn and dressed in black. And there's always a lot of work needing to be done."

"Ask her if her friends like their jobs any better," suggested Dilly.

XT did and Charlene admitted that they probably didn't. "We'd all like to be ladies," she said with a self-deprecating smile.

"Would you miss your family if you left Prosper Station?"

"I'd miss them awful and I know they'd be unhappy. I'm their only child."

"Suppose Daniel doesn't have to leave town. Is there some way you could get married and still keep your jobs?"

"We'd have to wait until Daniel found a place for us both to live."

"Would that be so terrible?"

Charlene shrugged.

"Do you think Mrs. Isbister would keep you on after you married?"

"Probably. At least until I started having children."

"And then you'd stay home and care for them."

"I'd have a garden and raise chickens to help feed us all," she said.

"So it could all work out," said XT.

"I guess," she smiled.

"Who are you talking to out there, Charlene?" asked Malcolm opening the door from the front hall.

"It's a man wondering if we need more water," said Charlene quickly.

"But the water man was here yesterday," said the boy. "Oh, the women are back again!" he exclaimed. "Are you going to stay here again?"

"We can't," said Azur.

"He's got such an imagination," Charlene explained to XT, shaking her head.

Overhearing conversation at the front door, Alice left the piano to investigate.

"Look, Alice, the ladies are back," said Malcolm to his sister. "And they brought a cat!"

"I see the cat," said the girl. "But I don't see any ladies."

"There are no ladies," said Charlene. "Just a nice gentleman."

"I'll be on my way now, Miss Murray," said the doctor. "Best of luck to you."

"Goodbye, Mister," said Malcolm. "Goodbye, nice ladies. Goodbye, pretty cat."

"Goodbye, young man," said XT.

Dilly and Azur waved and blew kisses.

"Mrroow!" said Bleu, twisting herself around Malcolm's legs.

The boy laughed delightedly.

"You handled that really well, Dr. Barkley," said Azur as the exceptional quartet strolled back to Johnson House.

"I have lots of talents," said XT, reaching for her hand.

Twenty-five

The lamp lighter had come and gone, leaving the streets of Prosper Station bathed in the soft glow of lamp circles. The town was further illuminated by a nearly-full moon which floated overhead in a night sky aglitter with stars.

"Lovely," sighed Dilly, gazing out from the window seat on which she sat.

"Too bad I have to break the spell by suggesting we go look for my sister," said Azur.

"That's what we're here for," said XT, resolutely rising from the settee. Bleu, who had been snuggling beside him, leapt to her feet and looked up expectantly.

"Although the idea terrifies me, I think we should try to enter Vapourlea tonight," said Azur.

"What do you have in mind?" asked XT.

"We need to go down to the hotel cellar."

"And wait for Vek to invite us in?"

"I believe so."

"My invitation came in the cellar of Tecumseh House," said Dilly, shuddering at the recollection.

"I wish I could call upon some moon magic for protection," said Azur.

"Why don't you?" asked XT.

"Whenever Mavis mentioned moon magic in our presence, Bram would give her warning coughs and raised eyebrows. I don't know if she was ever into lunar chants or spells but certainly Hilma and I weren't taught any."

"It's a pity," said Dilly. "We could sure use some spells and chanting. Think back, though, and tell us everything you managed to pick up about lunar potencies because you never know what might help."

"Alright. The moon travels through various cycles and moves through astrological signs more rapidly than the sun."

"Go on!"

"Spells are cast according to moon phase. We've been in the phase of waxing moon magic ever since we got here."

"What's significant about this phase?" asked Dilly.

"From what I remember, the phase of the waxing moon is a time for constructive magic in areas of friendship, health, success and courage."

"Perfect!" said Dilly.

"You've been rather quiet, XT," said Azur. "What are you thinking?"

"I'm thinking that all this talk about moon magic is rather witchy and I can see why people wondered about Mavis and my Aunt Janet."

"This is not a time for jest," scolded Azur.

"I'm only half jesting," said XT. "After all, here we are in Prosper Station with psychic vampires and other mutants."

"And Bleu," said Dilly.

"Mrrooow," purred the cat.

"Okay, let's get serious," said XT. "We do know that the earth is greatly influenced by the cycles of the moon."

"Ocean tides, weather phenomena, animal and human behaviour, plant production," contributed Dilly.

"Exactly. So it's not a far stretch to believe that sensointuitives have the ability to draw upon lunar power," said XT.

"With this being the phase of friendship, success and courage, it should be a good time to rescue Hilma," said Dilly.

"Don't forget the *health* aspect Azur mentioned," added XT. "Combined with success and courage, that would indicate we have a good chance of getting out with life and limb."

"If only Zhiab would provide some of his wisdom right about now," sighed Azur.

"I am at your service," said the guardian quietly, standing in the middle of the room.

"Zhiab!" cried Dilly.

"Oh, Zhiab," said Azur. "I'm terrified of Vek's power over me."

"With good reason," said Zhiab. "You must not enter Vapourlea until you have mastered the art and science of fully liberating your powers."

"Am I capable of doing this?" moaned Azur.

"Believe in yourself," said Zhiab. "You are making steady progress towards mastery."

"Progress," echoed Azur dismally.

"Keep your attention closely fixed on your sensointuitive powers as you would on a lamp shining in a dark place."

"But I'm not a Buddhist lama or a cloistered nun!"

"There are many besides monastics who master total concentration."

"But is there time?"

"Because of your exceptional abilities, the time you have is sufficient."

"Tell me what I must do," she pleaded.

"The darkness is never darkness to the One. This is your mantra. Repeat it."

Azur repeated his words carefully. "The darkness is never darkness to the One. The darkness is never darkness to the One."

Zhiab gave his head a single nod.

"I'd rather recite Keats," said Dilly. "It's more sensuous."

"You may do that, Miss Dillian," said Zhiab. "It's all about fixed attentiveness. You must not let your mind wander for an instant while you are making your way through Vapourlea."

"Are there things we should know about that … place?" said Dilly.

"The caves and tunnels of Vapourlea wind their way beneath the town of Prosper Station in a series of mazes," said the guardian. "The Faefume lairs are distributed throughout."

"Mazes and lairs?" asked Azur. "As if tunnels and caves aren't enough!"

Zhiab nodded gravely. "Expect false starts and stops and be prepared to retrace your steps from time to time."

"But that means we'll have to memorize every step of the way including the dead ends and the retracing!" said Dilly.

"Which should be no problem," said Zhiab, "since memory is a natural sensointuitives aptitude."

"Aptitude takes on a whole new meaning when your life depends on it."

"Vek will try to take you directly to Hilma but you must resist this because you will not be able to find your way out of Vapourlea," said Zhiab.

"Where is the Vapour Gate?" asked Azur. "Dilly thought it was in the Tecumseh House cellars and yet Vek popped out of the cellars of Johnson House when I was down there."

"There are several Vapour Gates," said Zhiab. "You found two of them and there are others. One you may find useful is located below Fletcher House."

"Right across from Grand Trunk Railway Station," noted XT.

"I'm glad I didn't find it on my first night in Prosper Station," said Azur. "Of course I was too terrified to leave the maid's room that night much less prowl around in the cellars."

"You'd have come though if she'd needed you, Zhiab," said Dilly.

"I would have," said the guardian.

"Why did you not help my sister?" asked Azur.

"She made the choice to shun my guidance."

"Will you come to Vapourlea with us?" asked Dilly.

"Only another Sensointuitive has the power to rescue Hilma," said Zhiab.

"Are you saying you cannot enter Vapourlea?" asked Azur.

"This is a journey you must take."

"I'll be there, Az, with whatever powers I have," said Dilly.

"So will I," said XT.

"I'm sorry, Xavier Tennyson," said Zhiab. "You are not a Sensointuitive."

"But I have Bleu!"

"Bleu is an amazing catalyst. She enabled you to arrive in Prosper Station and she has indeed provided you with protection here. However, the chemistry between you and the cat is insufficient to counteract the evil energies in Vapourlea."

"I can't let Azur and Dilly go there without me!" said XT.

"I am sorry."

"Surely there's a way!"

"I will ponder the situation until I return two nights hence when the moon is full," said Zhiab.

October 29

Twenty-six

XT returned from lunch to report that Mae Witherton was not in the dining room.

"I'm going to pay her a visit," said Dilly, rising from the settee.

"I'll come along in case she needs nurse counselling," offered Azur.

The timeriders navigated the upper halls of Johnson House until they located Mae's room in the servants' quarters. Mae answered the door in her nightdress and held the door open for them to enter.

The room was furnished with a closet, two chairs and two small dressers which doubled as bedside tables for the two cots. Mae invited the timeriders to take the chairs while she sat on the edge of her bed. "My roommate be workin' so I can talk to you without lookin' like I be talkin' to meself."

"XT said you weren't in the dining room," said Dilly. "We came to see how you were."

"I was too weary to get dressed this mornin' so I was sittin' here feelin' sorry for meself," said Mae. "Then I got to readin' Harley's poem and weepin'. I could feel my Harley here beside me and hear his voice sayin' these words."

She picked up the worn, blood-stained paper from the dresser and read aloud:

"And when I feel, fair creature of an hour!
that I shall never look upon thee more,

never have relish in the faery power
of unreflecting love! - then on the shore
of the wide world I stand alone, and think
till love and fame to nothingness do sink."

At the end of the recitation as she sat on the cot in her shared little room, dressed in her nightdress, Mae Witherton sobbed inconsolably.

Azur and Dilly left their chairs to sit on either side of her, their arms around the little waitress' shaking shoulders.

"I believe you're unwell," said Azur when the weeping eased. "That's why you were too tired to get up and dressed for work."

"I do be feelin' rather poorly," said Mae.

"Your face is puffy and your legs and feet are swollen," said Azur. "Have you seen a doctor?"

"No."

"Will you let me take a look at you?"

"Are you a midwife?"

"I'm a nurse with extra training in several areas including babies."

"Alright then," said Mae.

"If you lie back, I can feel the wee one in your belly," said Azur.

Mae complied and the timerider floated her hands down the length of the young woman's body, lingering over areas where her innate sensors demanded additional information. Then she pressed her hands gently on the distended abdomen and felt through the thin cotton fabric for the size, condition and position of the foetus.

"You're carrying a lot of extra fluid and your blood pressure is slightly elevated," she reported.

"Is the baby doin' well?" asked Mae.

"Everything is still fine," Azur assured her. "You just have to stay off your feet as much as possible until the baby is born." She did not add that the woman had preeclampsia which, if untreated, could lead to seizures and be ultimately fatal to both mother and baby.

"Stayin' off my feet be impossible!" cried Mae, sitting up. "I have no choice but to keep workin'."

"Dilly, stay here with Mae while I go and see if Violet is in."

Her friend readily agreed and Azur set of for the Galvinston suite.

"May I come in?" she asked when Violet came to the door. "I need your advice."

"Of course," replied Violet.

She led Azur to the sitting room where Sean was playing solitaire at a cherry wood games table inlaid with mahogany and ivory. "Shall we stay here or would you rather talk privately in my room?"

"Here is fine," said the timerider.

"You're not at the hospital today," commented Azur once she and Violet were seated.

"I don't go there every day," said Violet. "Being blessed with financial independence, I have the luxury of choosing when to work."

"And I'm not at work because I'm basically lazy," said Sean.

"That's not true, of course," said his sister. "Sean is working on an important business deal from which he's taking a break."

"I'm glad you're home," said Azur, "because I need to consult with you about Mae Witherton,"

"I noticed that Mae wasn't in the dining room this morning," said Violet.

Azur described Mae's condition and was pleased to learn that the nineteenth-century nurse understood the seriousness of preeclampsia which she called *toxemia*.

"Clearly she must rest until the babe is delivered," said Violet.

"Unfortunately, she feels she cannot give up her job."

"Does she have family to care for her?"

"She has no one."

Violet briefly reflected in silence before saying, "Sean, what do you think about Mae Witherton staying with us for a while? I can have a cot brought up to my room for her."

"And after the baby is born?" he asked.

"Mae has a good aura and I'd like to keep her on as my personal maid if she's willing. It's only a matter of time before Barrington and I set up our own house. This emboldens me to speed up my decision. What do you say, Sean?"

Her brother considered the situation for a few moments before responding. "I'm okay with giving it a try," he said.

Violet smiled her appreciation at her brother who simply shrugged in response. They both knew that he often complied with his only sibling's requests.

"You were going to tell me about Barrington," Azur reminded Violet. "I'm dying to hear more."

"Yes, I did mention him to you when you visited the hospital," said Violet. "Well, Barrington Creswell is an oil producer recently arrived from the states. He's a self-made man as they say, and he's handsome, charming, well-spoken and mature. Furthermore, he loves me."

"Do you love him?"

"I do. He occupies my thoughts day and night."

"When you said that Barrington is mature, did you mean mature sensible or mature older?" asked Azur.

"He's twenty-seven," said Violet.

"Ooh, an older man," teased Azur.

"Like your doctor," smiled Violet.

"He's not my doctor," said Azur quickly.

"He should be," said Violet giving her a penetrating look.

When Azur remained quiet, Violet did not press for a response.

"Barrington wants to marry me as soon as possible," she continued, "and since I haven't known him long, I've been deliberating. Now, however, I feel destiny has spoken through Mae and I'm prepared to set an early spring date. This will still allow Sean and Barrington to make preliminary business plans."

"Sean and your fiancé are going into business together?" asked Azur.

"Yes, they're forming an oil production partnership. Barrington understands oil and Sean is the financial wizard."

"Careful with that word, *wizard*," said Sean.

"When are you prepared to have Mae move in with you?" asked Azur.

"What do you say, Sean?" queried his sister. "The hotel will let her go immediately if she's unable to work. And it's imperative that she be on bed rest from here on in."

"I guess she can move in whenever you wish."

"You're such an adorable big brother!" said Violet, crossing the room to give him a hug before turning to Azur. "Go tell Mae to pack her belongings and come here right away before my brother changes his mind," she said.

"I'll leave off the latter sentiment when I relay your generosity," said Azur, jumping up and rushing off to give Mae and Dilly the amazing news.

Twenty-seven

"I promise to not be makin' a nuisance of meself, Miss Galvinston," said Mae Witherton, putting her meagre belongings into a chest of drawers from which Violet had cleared her own clothing.

The hotel had provided a privacy screen, cot, bedside table and chair which, along with the chest of drawers, now occupied the far end of Violet's large room.

"On the contrary, your time with my brother and me will be well spent learning our ways and preferences," said Violet. "Then, when you and the baby move with me into my new home, it will be far simpler to include Mr. Creswell's ways and preferences."

"Who could have known the shadow people would bring me to you, Miss Galvinston, and that you would offer me a position in your household?"

"Speaking of shadow people, I've invited Azur and Dillian to drop by in the early afternoon to see your new setup. They'll not stay long because we all know how tired you are."

Leaving Mae to settle in, Violet joined her brother in the suite's sitting room where he was absorbed in business ledgers. No sooner had Violet picked up her needlepoint when she was interrupted by a firm knocking on the door.

"Message for you, Miss Galvinston," said the porter, handing her an envelope.

Violet thanked the porter, closed the door and read the note. "Sean," she said, turning to her brother, "Dr. Lougheed has sent me a note saying that he's releasing Daniel Racher from the hospital. Shall I order a carriage to pick him up and deliver him here?"

"Wouldn't a short walk in the fresh air do him some good?"

"Sean! The man has been kicked by a horse and has gashes and bruises!"

"As you please."

"I'll phone Dr. Lougheed from the lobby and let him know to expect the carriage. On my way back, I'll tell the timeriders to come early so they're here for the occasion," said Violet.

"How did my life get so complicated in such a few days?" grumbled Sean.

"It's not good for one's constitution to become stagnant," smiled his sister as she left for the lobby.

A short time later, Violet escorted Mae Witherton to the sitting room. Wearing a robe and slippers provided by her new employer, the young woman already looked more refreshed. She nodded at Azur and Dilly who both smiled at her reassuringly.

"Have a seat right here, Mae," said Violet. "Have you met Daniel Racher?"

"I've seen him around town," said Mae, eying the young man with the bandaged arm.

"Daniel has something to tell you that should set your mind at ease," said Violet. "Go ahead, Daniel."

"I was there the day your husband was killed," said Daniel.

"You were at Tecumseh House?" asked Mae.

"Yes, I'd gone up to the second floor to tell Mr. Jarvis, one of the lodgers, his carriage was waiting below. It happened to be one of the occasions when Mr. Fletcher had me driving a carriage."

"You were actually there on the second floor?"

Daniel nodded. "There was no one at the lobby desk when I went in, so that's why I went upstairs myself."

"And what did you see?" asked Mae.

"Well, I heard some cries and moans in one of the rooms so I kind of froze, wondering what was going on in there. Just then Mr. Witherton came up the stairs carrying a paper package. He entered the room where the noise was coming from and I heard him shout, 'Stop!'"

"What happened next," prompted Sean.

"I peeked through the open door to see if Mr. Witherton needed help. Loreena Dales who works at Tecumseh House was standing over someone lying in the bed all covered with blood. She had a knife in her hands and Mr. Witherton was trying to get it away from her."

"Go on," prompted Violet.

"That was when Mr. Dunn, another lodger, came running out of his room two doors down and pushed me aside. 'Murderer!' he yelled into the room. Then he ran back to his room and returned with a gun. I heard a shot and I thought he'd killed Loreena since she was the one with the knife. But then I heard him asking Loreena what she was doing there and I knew he'd mistaken Mr. Witherton for the killer."

"So you didn't see my Harley being shot?' asked Mae.

"No, because I stayed out in the hall after Mr. Dunn pushed me out there."

"Why didn't you tell the police?" cried Mae, tears streaming down her face.

"Daniel's story isn't finished yet," said Violet gently. "Tell Mae what happened next, Daniel."

"I could hear Loreena crying and saying she did it because she loved Mr. Dunn and she didn't like all the time he spent with Julia, and Mr. Dunn said, 'You mean I shot an innocent man?' and he told Loreena she was a nobody and couldn't hold a candle to Julia who was a refined lady. Then Loreena said, 'You're the one who shot him,' and Mr. Dunn said, 'Look what you've got me into.'

Daniel became quiet and sat with his head in his hands, overcome by the recollection of that horrible day. The only sounds in the room were the ticking of the mantle clock and an occasional sniffle from Mae. Finally he continued.

"Loreena said that since the man was already dead and had blood all over his hands, there'd be no harm in blaming Julia's stabbing on him. She said she'd just put the knife beside his body. Then I heard her say, 'Look, a love poem. Guess you weren't the only one in love with Julia.'"

"It wasn't that way at all, Daniel," said Mae. "Julia Simpson was an invalid and my Harley used to read to her sometimes when he brought tonic to her from the pharmacy."

Daniel nodded in sympathy. "Shall I finish my story?" he asked her.

"Yes," she said. "I have to hear it all."

"I heard Mr. Dunn say, 'You won't get away with this,' and Loreena said, 'We're in this together, darling,' and Mr. Dunn said, 'You're not my darling.' Well, then I noticed Mr. Jarvis standing in the hall looking shocked. I think he'd been standing there for a while. He's the man who ordered the carriage and who I went upstairs for in the first place. He beckoned to me and whispered, 'Are you the livery boy?' I told him, 'Yes, Sir,' and he grabbed my arm and pulled me toward the stairs. Just as we started down, I looked back and there was Mr. Dunn glaring at us from the doorway where the killings happened."

"Did he say anything?" asked Mae.

"He didn't have a chance because Mr. Jarvis said, 'Hurry up, boy!' and I ran down the stairs after him. When we reached the lobby, Mr. Jarvis told me to never talk to anyone about what we'd seen."

"Did the police question you?" asked Mae.

"No," said Daniel. "They wouldn't know I'd been at Tecumseh House that day unless Mr. Jarvis told them. And I think he was too frightened by what he'd heard."

He looked sadly at Mae. "I'm really sorry about Mr. Witherton. He was a good man who everybody liked. I didn't know until yesterday that he had a wife or I'd have come to you sooner."

Mae gave a slight nod.

"Ever since the killings, I've been living in fear," Daniel continued. "I reached the point where I couldn't stand it anymore and I've been planning to leave town."

"You don't have to leave town now," said Sean. "After you told your story to Violet and XT in the hospital yesterday, Dr. Lougheed called the police."

"So Loreena Dales and Edward Dunn are in gaol?" asked Mae.

"Unfortunately, they managed to skip town," said Sean. "The police think someone tipped them off."

"So I'm still not safe," said Daniel.

"Now that the truth is out, they have no reason to come after you," said Sean. "No doubt they've crossed the border into the United States."

"Where they'll live happily ever after," said Mae.

"No danger of that," Azur assured her. "We saw them both when XT was breakfasting at Tecumseh House our second day here, and Edward Dunn clearly disliked Loreena Dales."

Aware that Daniel was not privy to the timerider's input, Sean added for his benefit, "Not only are they accomplices to murder, they'll be fugitives from the law for the rest of their miserable lives."

"How do you feel about all this, Mae?" asked Violet.

""I'm happy my Harley's name be finally cleared."

"He was a hero," said Dilly.

Mae nodded, her eyes bright with tears.

Twenty-eight

"It's good you've solved your family murder mystery, Dillian," said XT after he had been filled in on the events of the afternoon. "Now you'll be able to tell your family that your great-great grandfather was a brave, kind man."

"Best of all, Mae knows his name has been cleared," said Dilly. "She always believed in him."

"I wonder why the real story wasn't handed down through your family," said Azur.

"I've been musing over that too. I suppose since Loreena Dales and Edward Dunn eluded trial, there'd be no court records."

"I'm sure Mae told her son the truth about his father, but over time, the story must have faded from family lore," said Azur.

"Unfortunately, even today when people's names are cleared, it's not considered newsworthy enough to attract media attention," said XT. "Harley Witherton's after-the-fact innocence might not have made the *Prosper Station Topic*."

"Do you know if Mae had any other children?" asked Azur.

"That much I do know," said Dilly. "My great-great grandfather was an only child. His mother never remarried, and in her later years, she opened a millinery shop."

"You know, Azur, you haven't said anything about Mavis' ancestors," said XT. "What was their surname?"

"My grandmother's maiden name was McConnel," said Azur.

"If she's a true Senso and not an import like the Galvinstons, her family must have lived here during this time period."

"I feel badly that I haven't looked them up, but I have so little time as it is," said Azur.

"I'm sure Mavis would be pleased if you could tell her some little thing about them," said XT.

"Especially since you've spent so much time with Bram's ancestors," said Dilly.

"You're both right," said Azur. "Tomorrow when I talk to Violet about auras, I'll ask her if she's met any McConnels since she moved to Prosper Station."

"Why are you talking to Violet about auras?" asked XT.

"I heard her tell Sean that Mae had a good aura, and I got the impression that the subject of aura reading was commonplace to them."

"Would you mind if I go with you for that conversation?" asked XT. "Apart from the glow I've seen around Bleu, I've not had much opportunity to study emanations here."

"By all means come along," said Azur. "It goes without saying that you'll be there too, Dil."

"I should hope so!" said Dillian.

"I'm going down shortly to join the Galvinstons in the dining room," said XT. "Sean's invited me to drop by afterwards to play chess with him," said XT.

"Mrrooow," said Bleu.

"I wouldn't dream of going without you," said XT to the cat.

"Enjoy yourself," said Azur.

"You don't mind that I'll be later than usual getting back?"

"Take your time," said Dilly. "Azur and I will be rehearsing our mantras."

After XT and Bleu left, the timeriders practiced their mantras as Zhiab had advised. Soon they turned to discussing emanations.

"Can you see my aura?" asked Azur.

"Faintly. It seems to be purplish blue and green."

"You have a double one too," Azur told her friend. "I can see pale wisps of violet and yellow around you."

"I wonder if the paleness means our auras are weak or that our perception of them is," said Dilly.

"Perhaps it means both," said Azur. "Hopefully Violet will know."

"Now that we've dutifully practiced mantras and contemplated auras…" said Dilly.

"… and have determined that we need help with the latter…"

"… how should we spend the remainder of the evening?"

"We *could* go to the cellar and see if we can locate the Vapour Gate," said Azur.

"That way we'll be more prepared when Zhiab gives us the go-ahead," agreed Dilly.

"I think I remember where it was and we might be able to see a mark or indentation in the wall."

"On our other encounters with Vek, we were alone," said Dilly. "With the two of us present, we'll be able to stand our ground."

Azur and Dilly made their way to the hotel's summer kitchen and descended the stairs to the cellar.

"It's really quiet down here," said Dilly shivering. "I'm glad the wall lamps are still burning."

"Right about now I'd welcome some servants making out behind the trunks," said Azur.

"Pardon?"

"They were here the last time I was," said Azur.

"Okay…" said Dilly quizzically.

"Anyway, right over here is where Vek appeared."

The timeriders moved cautiously towards the place where Azur previously saw the wall close over the Faefume's fading form.

"The cave mouth was somewhere around here," said Azur.

"The wall looks pretty solid now," said Dilly. "We should probably get back upstairs in case XT returns and worries about us," she added nervously.

As the women prepared to leave, a subtle movement in the wall caught their attention. When a small chink between foundation stones widened steadily into a gaping hole, the timeriders gasped and clutching each other's arms.

Two forms emerged slowly from the blackness. One was Vek, green and haughty, the other was a thin, fragile girl with pale green skin who walked like a sleepwalker, a dreamy expression on her face.

"Hilma?" asked Azur, uncertainly.

"Azur!" cried the girl. "I knew you would come."

However, when Azur stepped closer to the cave mouth, Vek and Hilma backed slowly away, distancing themselves from the entrance.

Dilly held Azur's arm firmly. "Be careful," she warned.

"I need you, Azur. Don't leave me here alone," pleaded Hilma as the wall sealed itself over the shrinking dark cavity.

"She was so close," said Azur, tears spilling down her face.

Dilly placed a comforting arm around her friend's shoulders. "We'll get her, Az," she said.

"Did you notice their auras, Dil?"

"Hilma's was white," said Dilly. "And Vek's was a murky mustard colour surrounded by black. Is that what you saw?"

"Yes."

"See, we're getting better," she said, smiling weakly. "I think Zhiab will be pleased."

October 30

Twenty-nine

"I'm totally freaked," said Azur as she and Dilly waited for XT to return from breakfast. "It's already October thirtieth!"

"I'm a bit edgy myself," said Dilly. "Of course, I'll be even twitchier tonight when there's a full moon."

"What's this about a full moon?" asked XT, entering the suite.

"I was just saying that …" said Dillian

"Is Violet back in her suite?" Azur interrupted.

"You *are* eager," said XT.

"I'm not eager, I'm bordering on hysteria," said Azur. "Tomorrow is All Hallow's Eve and at the stroke of midnight marking the beginning of All Saints Day, we have to be boarding the train from hell with my sister."

"Close your eyes and take a few slow breaths," advised XT.

"I've been taking deep, slow breaths all morning," said Azur.

"More like hyperventilating," commented Dilly.

"Do you suppose Violet and Sean know about Vapourlea?" Azur wondered.

"Not likely," said XT. "We're in nineteenth-century Prosper Station and sensointuitive people, along with Vapourlea, are still evolving."

"Well, they know *something* about it," said Azur. "Mabel Isbister spoke of ghost visitors and shadow people, and she told me that this time last year she saw a girl – probably Hilma - in their back yard. Furthermore, she said that when ghost visitors disappear before the Hallowmas train returns for them, it's because something bad has happened."

"Undoubtedly sensointuitive townsfolk are aware of the presence of evil," said Dilly, "but I've never come across archival evidence indicating they knew of a place called Vapourlea."

"Violet and Sean seem to have arrived in Prosper Station already endowed with hypersensory attributes," said Azur.

"Which is why their father sent then from Salem," XT reminded her. "After his wife's death, he feared further repercussions resulting from the family's reputation."

"Are you saying they're witches?" asked Azur.

"*I'm* not," said XT, "but certainly they have attributes that superstitious people might associate with witchcraft."

"I don't believe the Galvinstons are witches," said Dilly.

"Why thank you for not calling Bram a witch," said Azur.

Dilly smiled at the sarcasm in her friend's voice. "From what I know of Bram, he's probably merely a *carrier* of whatever capabilities run in the family."

"Whereas I am a true product of whatever–it–is."

"Exactly."

"Okay ladies, I believe it's time to go calling on Sean and Violet," interrupted XT.

Moments later, Violet opened the door to her suite with a welcoming smile and led the visitors to her sitting room. "Sean has left for work and Mae is resting," she informed them.

"Thank you for seeing us," said Azur.

"My pleasure," said Violet.

"We're hoping you can give us information on auras," said Azur. "I heard you tell Sean that Mae had a good one."

"Are you interested in Mae's aura?"

"We're interested in what auras mean and how we can develop our ability to interpret them," explained Dilly.

"Perhaps you can tell me what you already know," said Violet.

"Dilly and I can see auras but they're very faint," said Azur.

"What does Dilly's aura look like to you?"

"It's violet and yellow."

"Indeed it is. Yellow reflecting her wisdom and enthusiasm for life and violet for her spiritual and artistic qualities. And Dr. Barkley's?"

"XT's aura is green and orange."

"Ah, yes. Green for compassion, reliability and healing. Orange for courage, competence and physical desire." Violet's eyes travelled between Azur and XT and she smiled. "What about yours, Azur?" she asked.

"Dilly tells me that mine is green and purplish blue."

"Green and *indigo*, wouldn't you say, Dilly?"

"Indigo, of course," corrected Dilly, the artist. "I see it so indistinctly that the exact colour is difficult to confirm."

"As with XT's aura, Azur's green relates to compassion, reliability and healing," said Violet. "Indigo, though, is very special. It reflects wisdom, insight, intuition and ultimately, *the third eye*."

"The third eye?" asked Azur.

"Mystical enlightenment which exists beyond the insight and intuition you already possess. It will grow with you over your lifetime as you become increasingly familiar with it. You may experience flashes of it even now at times when you need it most."

"I hope so," said Azur.

"Why are auras so hard to see?" asked Dilly.

"Most people can't see them at all," said Violet. "It's an inherited aptitude that requires nurturing and training. You and Azur have been ignoring this wonderful gift you have. You both have the capacity to perceive auras in a much richer way than you presently do."

"How large is an aura?" asked XT.

"Normally, two to three feet on all sides, above the head and below the feet into the ground. The healthier you are physically and spiritually, the more vibrant your energy field is and the further an aura extends."

"Can things that are spiritually *un*healthy emit auras?" asked Dilly.

"You speak of evil," noted Violet. "Yes. Fortunately, such beings are exposed by the nature of their auras."

"Whenever Bleu senses evil or danger, she and XT are surrounded by a single pale blue aura," said Azur.

"Remarkable," said Violet. "Pale blue indicates devotion, truth and survival."

"Mrrooow," said Bleu.

"Please tell us whatever you think we should know," said Dilly. "We have very little time."

Violet gazed upon the timeriders with sympathy. "You're going to have to trust me and provide me with more information," she said. "I know that you're from a different place and time. Let's start with you, Dr. Barkley. Do you bring medical knowledge of this from where you're from?"

"There is a growing body of neurological evidence of auras where we come from," said XT. "Aura readers have been able to observe changes in the human energy field prior to brain wave recordings registering changes in blood pressure measurements, galvanic skin responses, heart beat and muscle contractions."

Violet nodded with awed comprehension.

"Neurobiologists have discovered that emotionally-charged thoughts and experiences cause the body to manufacture chemicals called neuropeptides," said XT.

"I'm not at all surprised," said Violet.

Encouraged by her surprising grasp of what he was telling her, XT continued. "There's a medical condition called synesthesia in which brain regions responsible for processing each type of sensory stimuli are abnormally interconnected.

Some people with this condition associate colours with face recognition, numbers and alphabet letters."

"Interesting," commented Violet.

"Others actually experience the sensations of touch or pain that are occurring in persons they are observing," said XT.

"These people would possess a high degree of empathy," said Violet.

"They do," said XT.

"I would expect to find this diagnosis in some artists and healers," said Violet.

"You amaze me," said XT.

"Perhaps now *you* will trust me, Azur. Why did you come to Prosper Station?" asked Violet.

Azur took a deep breath and turned to the woman whom she believed to be her great-great aunt. "I'm here to bring back my sister from an evil place called Vapourlea where she is being held by a psychic vampire."

"Do you have evidence of this?"

"Dilly and I have both seen, with our own eyes, my sister in the company of the vampire."

"Where did this occur?"

"In the cellar."

"Of Johnson House?"

"Yes, a hole opened in the wall and they were standing there."

"Can you describe them for me?"

"Hilma, my sister, looked pale and fragile. She was surrounded by a white aura," said Azur.

"And Vek, who is a Faefume, is green in colour," said Dilly. "His aura is black nearest his body and a mustard colour as it goes outward."

"Vek is a psychic vampire?"

"Yes," said Azur. "And if it wasn't for Zhiab, we would be his captives by now."

"Zhiab is another Faefume?" asked Violet.

"Quite the opposite!" said Azur. "Zhiab is a Novapetrol, a guardian. He's blue with a purplish blue aura."

"Indigo," said Violet. "You are fortunate to have his help."

"You believe us," said Azur, relieved.

"I have no reason to doubt you," said Violet. "After you visited the Lougheed hospital, the patient with stomach cancer announced she was hungry. Her entire appearance is changing and I believe she's on the mend. Moreover, the railway brakeman's face is healing at an amazing rate. It looks as if the scarring will be minimal, which is incredible for burns as severe as his."

"That's wonderful," said Azur.

"Did you touch those people?" asked Violet.

"I did touch that poor woman. She was suffering so much. And, as we were leaving, I brushed against the burn patient on the verandah," said Azur, looking bemused.

"You are a gifted healer," said Violet.

Warmed by this affirmation of her increasing powers, Azur smiled her gratitude.

"Do you wish to know the meaning of your sister's aura?" asked Violet.

"Yes," said Azur hesitantly.

"White reflects dependence on an addictive substance," said Violet. "It is also the aura of someone who is near death."

Azur, Dilly and XT remained silent.

"As for the Faefume, mustard is indicative of a manipulative nature while a black aura is the colour of an energy vampire. This being is very dangerous."

The timeriders nodded solemnly.

"How do you plan to rescue Hilma?"

"Zhiab tells us we must enter Vapourlea and search for her through the tunnels and mazes. He says we need to develop our powers in order to bring her out safely."

"Ah, yes," said Violet thoughtfully. "You're on the right path in seeking to study auras, for in developing that capability to its fullest, you will enhance *all* your faculties."

"Can you help us?" asked Dilly.

"I'll do whatever I can," she said. "To begin with, you must know that for an aura to be fully perceived and interpreted, all the senses must be activated including the sixth sense, intuition."

"Are you able to teach us this?"

"We're most fortunate that tonight the moon will be full and we can call upon her potency to aid you in your mission," said Violet. "One of the healers I've met in Prosper Station is gifted in lunar rituals and chants and I'll make certain she joins us tonight. Her name is Jane McConnel."

Thirty

Along the moon-lit streets of town, a horse-drawn carriage made its way to the residence of school master, George Tennyson, his wife, Sarah, and their three children. As soon as the carriage rolled to a stop at its destination, Violet Galvinston stepped down with the assistance of her companion, Dr. XT Barkley.

Three additional passengers alit from the carriage unobserved. One was a sleek silvery-blue cat who remained close to the physician's feet and the other two were timeriders, invisible to most.

As the horse and driver trotted back to the stalls at Scott's Livery, Violet led the newcomers along a stone pathway that wandered along the side of the house and thence into a hedged back garden through a wrought iron gate. The house was an Ontario cottage, similar in layout to that of the Lougheed home and private hospital, but its rooms were occupied by a lively family of five rather than by patients lying on clinical cots.

In the yard, two women, one in her early thirties, the other slightly younger, talked quietly while their children played nearby in a gazebo. When they noticed the visitors, they approached with smiles of welcome.

"These are the guests I told you about," said Violet to the women. "This is Dr. XT Barkley, a visiting physician with an interest in emanations. Our two lovely shadow people are Azur Moonstorey, a healer like the three of us, and Dillian Witherton, a talented intuitive."

"We were expecting you," said the younger of the two women. "I'm Sarah Tennyson. My children are playing over there with their friends."

"And I'm Jane McConnel," said the other woman. "Three of my seven children have accompanied me tonight and the others are home with my oldest daughter, Maeve."

"As you can imagine, the early darkness at this time of year is a bonus for our young ones since they can stay out *after dark*," said Sarah.

While the timeriders and the women exchanged pleasantries, two of the children silently left the gazebo to observe the visitors. They seemed especially interested in Azur and Dillian.

"These young lads are Roy McConnel and William Tennyson," said Violet.

"They seem to be the only ones of our collective ten children with the ability to see shadow people," said Sarah. "However, some of the other children are already showing intuitive aptitudes."

"I think we should begin our ceremony," said Jane. "It will soon be bedtime for the children."

"Have you participated in a lunar ritual before?" asked Sarah Tennyson.

"We haven't," said Azur, "and we're honoured that you so graciously invited us."

"Our visitors are seeking enlightenment about auras," said Violet, "and Azur and Dillian wish to enhance their aura-reading powers."

"This is the perfect time to do so," said Sarah. "The expert on channelling lunar power is Jane, but we will all contribute however we can."

"Perhaps for tonight, we can add explanations as we go along," said Jane. "The children will benefit from the lesson as well."

"Come, children," called Sarah softly. The children immediately left their play to join the adults.

"I'm the keeper of the gate tonight," announced the older of the Tennyson boys.

"Thank you, Robert," said his mother.

As the boy hurried toward his post, Sarah handed unlit candles to the participants. Jane picked up a lighted lantern and they followed her in single file to enter a circle of stone benches. She set down the lantern on a low marble pedestal in the middle of the circle and they all sat down facing the flickering light.

"Tonight is a special night," she said quietly to the seated circle of adults and children. "On this night of the full moon and until All Saints Day, the moon bestows on us heightened powers of prophesy, protection and divination. These powers will continue to grow within us through the knowledge we acquire in our dreams."

"Shall we begin?" asked Sarah.

Everyone nodded expectantly.

"Our mantra or chant is *The darkness is never darkness with the One*," instructed Jane.

Azur and Dillian exchanged surprised glances that residents of Prosper Station were familiar with Zhiab's mantra.

Jane raised her arms skyward and said. "We attribute all power to the One."

"The darkness is never darkness with the One," recited everyone in unison.

"We give thanks for the powers that flow from our Mother, the Moon," intoned Jane.

"The darkness is never darkness with the One," they chanted.

We have been blessed with a healing ministry," said Jane. "May we be bearers of hope, serenity and inner peace."

"The darkness is never darkness with the One."

"We pray to be vessels of joy in the midst of suffering," said Jane.

"The darkness is never darkness with the One."

Jane gestured with downward-facing palms that they should sit. "Remove your footwear," she instructed.

They seated themselves upon the stone benches and set their candles beside them to remove shoes and stockings. "We remove our footwear to feel beneath our feet the power of the earth's magnetism and energy," explained Sarah in a conversational voice.

Jane raised her hands palm-upward signalling that they should rise. She faced westward and the others did likewise.

"Earth is the element of building, learning and history," said Sarah. "It is the place of birth, death and transformation."

"We turn to the West, the direction of the setting sun, to invoke the power of Earth," intoned Jane in a slow, tranquil voice. "May we receive through the blessings of Earth, the gifts of wisdom and intuition," intoned Jane.

"The darkness is never darkness with the One," chanted the small assembly.

Jane placed her hand over her heart and turned to face south as did the participants.

"The element of water generates and nurtures all life," explained Sarah. "It mirrors our emotions, is flexible and flowing."

"We turn to the South, the direction of the heart, to invoke the power of Water," intoned Jane. "May we receive through the blessings of Water, the gifts of wisdom and intuition."

"The darkness is never darkness with the One," they chanted.

Sarah retrieved the lantern from the middle of the circle and went from person to person allowing each to light their candle from the lantern. Lastly, she lit her own, returned the lantern to its former place and returned to her place. "The element of Fire is the creative energy of light and life," she explained.

"We turn to the East, direction of the rising sun, to invoke the power of Fire," intoned Jane as they all turned eastward. "May we receive through the blessings of Fire, the gifts of energy, illumination and healing."

"The darkness is never darkness with the One," they chanted.

Jane held her hands before her in prayer position and turned to the north. Everyone turned northward, hands in prayer position.

"Air is the breath of life," said Sarah. "It is the element which enables the co-existence of fire and water."

"We turn to the North, the direction of wisdom, to invoke the power of Air," intoned Jane. "May we receive through the blessings of Air, the gifts of intuition and the powers essential to psychic work."

"The darkness is never darkness with the One," they chanted.

"The vibration of chant sets up forces for purifying and refining our magnetic fields," said Sarah.

"The power of sound changes the auras for healing and higher consciousness," added Jane. "Since we build up our auric fields by chanting, we will continue to chant until we feel ourselves infused with moon energy."

She walked slowly from within the circle and proceeded to move clockwise around the outside of the stone benches. Holding their lighted candles before them, they walked round and round, intoning their chant: "The darkness is never darkness with the One… the darkness is never darkness with the One… the darkness is never darkness with the One… the darkness is never darkness…"

Still chanting, they followed her back to their seats and became silent.

"Close your eyes and meditate with the energy of the full moon upon you," she said quietly. Everyone sat in silence, eyes closed, the energy of the moon touching them with feathery fingers.

"Absorb the energy of the earth beneath your feet." They pressed their bare feet into the grassy earth, feeling the energy rising upward through their limbs.

"Breathe deeply and slowly, drawing in the air that surround you." All breathed deeply and slowly of the autumn night air.

"Quiet your minds and channel the information that comes to you through the energy of water and fire." Their senses were vibrant with the energy of the elements coursing through their bodies.

"Hold out your arms before you with palms facing upward, and wait for the lunar energy to fill you." For several minutes, they remained in silent meditation, absorbing the powers of the universe in the embrace of the full moon's powers.

"Mama, we have a visitor!" called out Robert, the keeper of the gate.

Immediately, the children rose from the circle and snatched the candles from the adults' hands. They extinguished them as they ran to the gazebo.

"Stay where you are," Violet told the timeriders calmly. "Sarah will attend to the *visitor*.

Sarah walked briskly to the gate. "Good evening, Officer Ferguson," she said pleasantly. "Are you making rounds?"

"Sorry to bother you, Mrs. Tennyson," said the policeman. "One of your neighbours was concerned that there was a problem here."

"Since when is it a problem to have a few friends over on a beautiful autumn night?" asked Sarah.

"Ah, yes," said the policeman. "And the moon so round and full in the starry skies."

"So lovely," agreed Sarah mildly. "Would you like to meet my guests?"

"If you don't mind," said Officer Ferguson.

Sarah Tennyson escorted the man into her hedged garden. He looked carefully around and saw children playing in a gazebo. He observed two women, Jane McConnel and Violet Galvinston, casually sitting on garden benches in the company of a young man who shared his bench with a silvery blue cat.

"I don't believe you've met Dr. Barkley," said Sarah as XT rose and came over to shake the policeman's hand.

"New in town, are you, Doctor?" asked the policeman.

"Just passing through," said XT. "I'm staying at the Johnson House."

"It would seem that all is well here," said John Ferguson, tipping his cap as he departed into the night.

Thirty-one

Jane McConnel walked over to the gazebo where the children were talking excitedly in hushed tones about their recent escape from detection by Officer Ferguson. She addressed twelve-year-old Blanche and ten-year-old Gertie. "Girls, please hitch up the carriage. It's time for us to go home."

The children sighed.

"I'll bring the lantern to the barn," offered Robert Tennyson. At nine, he was the oldest of George and Sarah Tennyson's three children.

As Blanche, Gertie and Robert walked towards the small barn which the Tennyson menagerie of horse, pony and chickens was temporarily sharing with the McConnel horse, the other children left the gazebo and began to skip around the stone garden benches.

"Let's go sit in the gazebo while the children are otherwise occupied," said Sarah Tennyson.

XT, Azur and Dillian accompanied Violet and Jane as they followed their hostess to the gazebo. When they were all seated, Jane looked expectantly at the visitors.

"Apart from the abrupt finale created by Officer Ferguson's arrival, what did you think of the evening?" she asked.

"Most informative," said XT. "Of course, I'm not gifted with the special powers the others have so I didn't get the full effect."

"It was wonderful," said Azur. "I can already perceive auras more clearly."

"The colours of auras are radiant!" said Dilly. "I had no idea."

"You will find auras extremely helpful in your healing ministry, Azur," said Jane. "You and Dillian will both perceive people and situations in an entirely new way."

"Keep in mind that auras are perceived objectively with the physical eye as well as intuitively with the mind's eye," said Jane.

"Remember what I told you about the third eye," Violet reminded her.

Azur nodded numbly.

"The visitors have a special reason for needing the power provided by auras," said Violet to Jane and Sarah. "Are you prepared to expand your own realm of knowledge by hearing what they have to say?"

"I'm intrigued," said Jane.

"As am I," said the hostess.

Azur explained her quest for her sister. She told the women about mutants, Faefumes and Novapetrols. She described Vek and Zhiab and spoke of her terror at having to search for Hilma in the tunnels, caves and mazes of Vapourlea. The women listened in amazement.

"We have seen the shadow people," said Sarah, "and we sensed that they were in peril from something sinister. But we were unaware that there was such a place as Vapourlea in a dimension existing beyond our experience."

"It's just as well," said XT. "Vapourlea and mutants are not meant to be part of our daily reality."

That's true of both the nineteenth century and *ours,* thought Azur.

I heard that! responded XT, turning to Azur in surprise.

"Are you engaged in thought sharing?" asked Jane of the timeriders.

"I don't know," said Azur. "Do you know what we were thinking?"

"No," said Jane, "but I could feel the exchange of mind energy between the two of you."

"It's a gift that's shared by a few kindred souls," said Violet. "The moon has smiled on you."

"Since you must soon go to that frightening place to rescue your sister, keep rehearsing what you learned tonight," said Jane.

"You sound like Zhiab," said Azur.

"Zhiab must be a wonderful guardian," said Sarah.

Azur nodded.

"As you contemplate your quest, maintain a clear vision of your goal," said Jane. "Always keep the image of a successful rescue in your mind. More importantly, you must connect with a different consciousness."

"The soul consciousness linking every human being with celestial energy," explained Violet.

"I don't understand what you're saying," said Azur dismayed.

"You will understand when the time is right," Sarah assured her.

"Did you say that there is a Vapour Gate at the Fletcher House?" asked Jane.

"Yes."

"Use that gate exclusively because it's right across from the Grand Trunk Railway which once owned it," said Jane. "My husband, James, is a GTR railway conductor and he will help you board the train with your sister."

"Is he a Senso?" asked Dilly.

"Pardon?"

"We call people with enhanced sensory and intuitive abilities, *Sensointuitives*," explained XT."

"Sensos, for short," said Azur.

"They're the ones who can see shadow people," added XT.

"Oh, like Jane and me," said Sarah.

"In answer to your question, Dilly, I'd describe my husband as having limited sensory and intuitive abilities," said Jane.

"However, he *can* discern the presence of shadow people in a hazy way and, more importantly, he is able to communicate with the conductor on the Hallowmas train."

"Are they friends?" asked Azur.

"Not friends, but they have a tolerant business relationship."

"Mama, I'm tired," said Gertie. "We have the horse and carriage ready to go."

"I must leave now," said Jane.

"Let's meet here tomorrow evening when we're all in costume for our All Hallows Eve party," said Sarah. "We'll accompany XT and the shadow people to the Vapour Gate and support their mission with our energy."

Reassured, the timeriders thanked their gracious mentors for the evening and for the promised support.

"I see our carriage pulling up now too," said Violet.

When Violet and the timeriders reached the Johnson House, only Violet entered the hotel. The others went walking at Azur's suggestion. "I'd like to locate the Vapour Gate at Fletcher House," she said, "so that I'm not as frightened tomorrow night."

"Are you sure it won't make you *more* frightened?" asked XT.

"I have to find it," she said.

"If you insist on doing this," said XT, "I'll at least be there to prevent any brash impulsiveness."

"Isn't that redundant?" asked Azur.

"I'm making a point."

No one noticed a man and a cat entering the Fletcher House lobby and walking confidently down the hotel halls leading to the rear. If they had, they would not have known that two invisible timeriders were in the lead.

The foursome located the cellar stairs and, leaving the door ajar at the top, descended to a room crammed with supplies. Then they heard conversational voices and the slamming of the cellar door, leaving them in total blackness.

"Maybe we should leave," said Azur. "We can't see a thing."

"I'll go first and make sure there's no one up there so that we can all slip out the back way," said Dilly.

Before she had a chance to move toward the stairs, one of the walls began to glow exposing a large hole that spread across the stone floor. Azur and Dilly tumbled into the hole but XT and a shrieking, electrified cat found themselves standing on an impenetrable glass–like surface.

In horror, XT could see beneath him a ramp leading down into darkness. "Azur! Dilly!" he called, but there was no reply.

He tried to recall what he had learned at the lunar ritual. *Connect with a different consciousness, the soul consciousness linking every human being with celestial energy.*

He focused intently on those words, willing his consciousness to reach into the tunnel. *Azur! Dilly! Cling to the celestial energy linking us together. Come towards me! Come Back!*

With a glimmer of hope, XT heard Azur's voice running through his mind. *I can hear you,* she cried. *Keep calling us!*

"Zhiab, you said you would return tonight. Where are you?" whispered XT. "We need you."

"I am here," said the Novapetrol, standing at XT's side. "Your friends have not gone far."

The guardian slipped through the glassy surface and returned with Azur and Dilly in his arms.

Enraged shrieks came from the blackness below and the floor sealed shut. "I thought you couldn't enter Vapourlea, Zhiab," said Azur.

"You were still in the antechamber of Vapourlea," replied the guardian. "It remains true that only you can rescue your sister."

The stone cellar was now comfortingly illuminated with the auras of Zhiab and the timeriders.

"I wish we could make light like this when you're not here," said Azur.

"You can," said Zhiab. "Focus on your sensointuitive powers as you would on a lamp shining in a dark place. Recite your mantra."

The Novapetrol kept his gaze on the timeriders until they chanted in unison, "The darkness is never darkness with the One… The darkness is never darkness with the One"

"What happened to Keats?" Zhiab asked Dillian.

"I've changed my mind," she said. "I feel more protected with your mantra. Besides, saying Azur's mantra will help us connect with the soul consciousness."

She was rewarded with a twinkle of approval in the guardian's dark eyes.

"Zhiab, you said you'd ponder my request to accompany Azur and Dillian to Vapourlea," said XT hopefully.

"I was concerned about your safety, but since you have demonstrated thought-sharing capabilities, I will help you pass through the Vapour Gate tomorrow night with your friends."

DAY 10

All Hallows Eve

Thirty-two

On All Hallows Eve, six of the seven McConnel children joined the three Tennyson children to celebrate at the Tennyson residence. Baby Russell McConnel had been left at home in the care of the family servant. The adults of both families were in attendance as were the Galvinstons, the timeriders, Mae Witherton and Violet's fiancé, Barrington Creswell.

Costumed in various interpretations of ghosts, saints, devils and angels, the children and adults gathered around a long table in the dining room. The table had been extended with table leaves and boards and was draped in pale green crepe paper. It was decorated with small Jack-o'-lanterns, dishes of candies and nuts, pyramids of fruits and platters of gingerbread.

The meal was served by the family domestic, Judith, who had brought in her sister, Esther, to assist with the festivities. The meal included witch's turnip and potato soup, goblin-face meat pies, ghoulish rarebit, orange jelly and orange-frosted cakes decorated with bats and ghosts.

"Why are there two empty chairs?" asked four-year-old Rhea McConnel.

"They're for the shadow people," said her sister, seven-year-old Lulia.

"Can *you* see them?" asked Rhea.

"No," admitted Lulia. "But Mama can."

Violet cast an anxious glance at Barrington who was seated between her and Sean. Her fiancé smiled and shrugged.

"Were you warned that you might be meeting some strange people here?" George Tennyson asked Barrington.

"Violet did mention that she and some of the people here tonight have special sensory abilities," said Barrington. "So tell me about the shadow people."

"It seems they arrive here by train in late October and leave again at midnight on All Saints Day," said George.

"Which is just a few hours from now," noted Barrington.

"That's right," said George.

"Do *you* see them?"

"No, but I try to keep an open mind. My wife, Sarah, who is admittedly a gifted healer, does, and so does my son, Robert. It's taken me a while to come to terms with this, but I have become a reluctant believer."

"Would you like to know who of us present tonight have the ability to see shadow people?" Sean asked his business partner and future brother-in-law.

"Sure," said Barrington. "I suppose *you* do?"

"Yes," said Sean.

"And you, Violet?"

When she nodded, he raised his eyebrows, saying nothing.

They went around the table and Mae Witherton, Jane McConnel and her son, Roy, also acknowledged seeing shadow people. The railway conductor, James McConnel, said that he could faintly detect shadow people but that he wasn't gifted in any other way. XT remained silent because he felt that explaining his strange catalytic relationship with a cat would be too much for the oil producer to handle.

"What do *you* think of all this, Dr. Barkley?" asked Barrington, seeking the opinion of the one other person who seemed new to these strange revelations.

"Like George, I'm trying to keep an open mind," said XT. "Within the medical world, there is a growing acceptance of people who possess intuitive healing abilities. There are also some who have demonstrated the ability to perceive magnetic energy fields around people and objects. So why not consider the existence of shadow people?"

Violet smiled at XT gratefully.

"Interesting," said Barrington. "Do séances and auras fit in with all this?"

"Magnetic fields are certainly related to auras," said the neurologist. "Can't say as I know much about séances."

"Do you still want to marry my sister?" asked Sean of his new partner.

"Sean!" said Violet, wishing she were close enough to give her brother a sharp nudge.

"It adds to her mystique," said Barrington, smiling at the lovely woman seated beside him. "I've already accepted that she's a healer, so I guess I can handle a few additional fascinating qualities."

"Good man!" said George Tennyson. "You'll get used to those *fascinating qualities* over time, you know, even if you never understand them. I speak from experience."

"If a school master can take this in stride, I guess an oilman can," said Barrington.

After dinner, the men retreated to the smoking room for cigars and cordials. The women took the children into the parlour to bob for apples, play Pin the Tail on the Donkey, and tell each other's fortunes.

"Sit down, everyone," said Jane when the games came to an end. "Sarah is going to tell us the story of how Hallowe'en came to be."

They gathered around, some sitting on chairs, sofas and ottomans, others sitting on the carpeted floor.

"The history of Hallowe'en dates back to the ancient Celtic festival of Samhain," said Sarah, pronouncing the festival as *sow-en*. "At that time, the Celts celebrated the new year on the first day of November, the day marking harvest and the beginning of the cold, dark winter months."

"When does it get to the scary part?" five-year-old Sadie asked her mother.

"Right now," said Sarah in a whispery voice.

The children shivered in delight.

"You see, on the thirty-first of October – that's today - the worlds of the living and the dead come together. The ghosts of the dead return to earth."

Leah squealed.

"Mrs. Tennyson is talking about what the ancient Celts believed," Maeve reassured her sister.

Sarah nodded and smiled.

"Go on. We want to hear the scary stuff," said William

"On this night the door to the Otherworld opens for the souls of the dead – as well as fairies - to enter our world."

"I hope I see a fairy tonight," said Sadie.

"Well, it has been called the festival of fairies," smiled her mother.

"Tell us about the bonfires," prompted Gertie.

"Ancient people let the hearth fires in their homes die out on this night so that they could relight them with sacred fire from the ceremonial bonfires," said the storyteller. "The entire village would gather around huge bonfires. They told fortunes and offered crops and animals to their deities."

"And they wore masks," prompted Sadie.

"Yes, people wore masks outside after dark to avoid being recognized by wandering ghosts who would mistake them for fellow spirits. They also placed bowls of food outside their doors to appease ghosts and keep them out."

"What would the ghosts do?" asked Lulia.

"They'd try to take you back to the Otherworld with them," said her brother, Roy, in an eerie voice.

The children gasped in delighted horror.

Sarah waited until her audience settled back for more story-telling. "Then, in the 800s, Christians decided to have celebrations on the same days that the Celtic pagans were appeasing the souls of the dead."

"I bet the Christians were afraid their children would join the pagan ceremonies," said Robert.

"Quite possibly," said Sarah. "Anyway, the first day of November was designated *All Saints' Day*, also called *All Hallows*, to honour the saints and martyrs."

"Hallows are saints?" asked Blanche.

"Correct, and that's why we call the night *before* All Hallows, *All Hallows Eve*."

"But we really call it Hallowe'en," said William.

"It's just another way of naming it," said his mother. "Shall I go on?"

"Yes!" said the children.

"Since the Church was honouring saints on the first day of November, it decided to honour the dead on the following day and called it *All Souls Day*. It was celebrated similarly to Samhain with bonfires, parades and costumes. The three celebrations combined, All Hallows Eve, All Saints Day and All Souls Day, is called Hallowmas."

"As in the Hallowmas train," said Azur to Dilly who nodded grimly.

Roy McConnel and William Tennyson, the only children able to see and hear the timeriders, exchanged wide-eyed glances.

"Can we go trick-or-treating now?" asked Rhea McConnel.

"Wait until Mrs. Tennyson finishes the story," said her mother, Jane, giving the child a stern look.

"We're getting to the end," said Sarah. "The tradition of trick-or-treating started with the English giving pastries called *soul cakes* to the poor in return for the promise to pray for dead relatives. This was considered better than leaving food and wine for roaming spirits. The practice was called *going a-souling*."

"And that's why we go trick-or-treating," said Rhea with four-year-old finality.

"It was a bit later when families gathered to tell ghost stories while eating nuts and apples, and children visited neighbourhood homes for ale, food and money," said Sarah, speeding up the story for her increasingly restless audience.

"Except that we don't get ale," said Sadie.

"Sometimes people give us apple cider," said Lulia.

The children were already milling about when Sarah called the gentlemen from the smoking room.

"XT has just informed us that he's leaving tonight and catching the midnight train," said Barrington. "We tried in vain to convince him to stay on a bit."

"Why don't we accompany Dr. Barkley to the Grand Trunk and make that our trick-or-treat route!" said Sarah gaily.

"Yes!" squealed the children, amazed at the prospect of adventuring beyond the usual neighbourhood houses.

"To the *station*? That's absolutely unsafe in the dark!" protested George.

"We'll carry lanterns," said Robert.

"We'll only go as far as Fletcher House," said Jane with a sideways glance at Azur and Dilly.

"Barrington and I are going back to Johnson House with Mae," said Sean. "I left instructions with Scott's Livery to pick us up any time now."

"Are you coming with us, Violet?" asked her fiancé.

"I'm going to help out with the children," she replied.

"I don't like the idea of ladies and children traipsing around downtown at this hour."

"It's Hallowe'en, Barrington!" said Violet.

"Drunks and prostitutes won't much care," he said.

"I'm helping out at the railway tonight," James McConnel assured him, "so I'll walk along with the ladies and youngsters."

"Dr. Barkley will be with us as well," said Jane.

"Have you given any thought about how you'll get home?" asked George.

"We'll take carriages, of course," said Sarah. "Fletcher Livery is right there."

"Nonetheless, I'm coming to Fletcher House with you," said George. "That way, when James and XT leave for the station, I can escort Violet across the street to the Johnson lobby. Then I'll hire carriages from the livery and get the ladies and children safely home."

Unaware of the pained glances exchanged by the women, George and Barrington congratulated themselves on having the matter well in hand.

Thirty-three

Carrying flickering lanterns and accompanied by a sleek, silvery cat, the masked and costumed trick-or-treaters made their way along the moonlit streets of Prosper Station. Their progress was determined by the time spent at each house visited by the children in the group.

Some people required that the children recite poetry or sing in exchange for the nuts, fruits and sweets they proffered. Others tried to guess the names of the nine youngsters peering at them from behind the masks. Some householders called out to the adults patiently waiting on the dirt roads.

Struggling to control the anxiety that gnawed at their stomachs, the timeriders tried to make light conversation with their nineteenth-century hosts. Nervously, they repeatedly checked that their precious return train tickets were on their persons. XT's fingers squeezed the soft bag containing his grandfather's gold coins and Azur was comforted by the smoothness of Bram's pocket watch nestled in her skirt pocket.

"I appreciate all you've done for us," said Azur to the healers.

"I will truly miss you," said Violet.

"When we start chanting at the hotel, take that as your cue to slip away and find your Vapour Gate," whispered Jane. "Carry with you the confidence that our lunar energies are united with yours."

Azur passed the instructions on to her timerider companions as the trick-or-treaters neared the lamp lit business section of town.

"I expect you have to retrieve your baggage from Johnson House," said George Tennyson to the doctor as they approached the crossroads of their destination.

"It's already been delivered to the station," said XT.

"In that case, I'll say good-bye to you now before I escort Violet across the street," said the school master, exchanging handshakes and warm wishes with his dinner guest.

"Come, Violet," said George, gallantly offering his arm to the young woman.

Violet looked at Sarah Tennyson for assistance in dealing with this awkward moment.

"George, dear," said Sarah, "we were hoping to make this evening special for the children. A full moon on All Hallows Eve is quite rare."

"And parading through the whole town hasn't been special enough?" asked George. "What more could you possibly have in mind?"

"I thought perhaps we could walk around Fletcher House and do a little chant," said his wife.

"Certainly not!" said George. "I will not be made to look a fool! And, if I'm not mistaken, the full moon was last night."

"Full moon magic lasts until All Saints Day," said Sarah.

"Don't let anyone hear you uttering such nonsense," said George, looking around warily.

"But it's Hallowe'en and we're all in costume," said Jane McConnel, coming to her friend's rescue. "It's all part of the atmosphere of this night."

"What do you think of all this, James?" asked George of the GTR conductor.

"I suppose there can be no harm in a walk-about," said James. "The children would enjoy it, I'm sure."

As the children clambered around their fathers, begging for permission to process around Fletcher House chanting, John Ferguson crossed the street on his rounds of downtown shops.

"Rather late to be downtown," observed the policeman. "The shops will be locking their doors any minute now."

"Just having a bit of fun with the children, John," said George. "We've been teaching them about the history of Hallowe'en."

"So typical of a school master," chuckled the policeman. "The lessons never stop."

"Officer Ferguson," said Jane McConnel gaily, "we were just about to parade around Fletcher House doing a little full-moon chant. Won't you join us?"

"Well, I don't know..." he spluttered.

"George and James are going along with it," added Jane quickly. "It would be such a lark if you would lead us!"

"Well, I suppose..." said the policeman uncertainly. "...provided we start soon because I have rounds to make. There's bound to be all sorts of mischief tonight."

"Let's start right now then!" said Lulia, smiling up at the policeman. "And let's go round and round the hotel!"

With Officer Ferguson grudgingly in the lead, they started walking around the hotel, holding their lanterns before them. The children giggled and whispered until the chant began.

"The darkness is never darkness to the One," intoned Jane.

"The darkness is never darkness to the One." Sarah and Violet joined in.

"The darkness is never darkness to the One... the darkness is never darkness to the One... the darkness is never darkness to the One... the darkness is never darkness to the One." The children added their voices to the chant.

"You're not saying it, Daddy," said Rhea to her father. Reluctantly he added his voice to the chant and soon the policeman and conductor were chanting too.

Shopkeepers and late customers planning to return home stopped by to watch the spectacle. Caught up in the fun, some joined the procession encircling the hotel.

With the sound of chanting in their ears, the timeriders slipped away unnoticed. They entered Fletcher House and descended to the cellar where Zhiab, true to his word, was waiting.

"You are ready," he reassured them. "Memorize every detail along the way so that you can retrace your steps. Remain united in celestial energy."

The timeriders hung intently on the Novapetrol's every word.

"And Azur," he said, turning his gaze upon her. "Turn on *all* your senses."

She nodded numbly.

"Shall we bring our lanterns?" asked XT when it seemed that Zhiab had no more to say.

"You'll have no need for them," said Zhiab.

Before they had a chance to reassess their anxiety levels, the wall began to glow. A crack near the base of the foundation expanded into the wall and spread across the floor. Hearts pounding, they backed up until the opening no longer reached towards them. Peering over the edge, they could make out a steep stone ramp that descended in flat shallow steps.

"Go confidently," said Zhiab.

Cautiously, they helped each other through the opening, Bleu never more than a few inches from XT's feet. Huddled together, the timeriders walked down the ramp. They followed it around a corner where it levelled off into a wide path between high walls of striated taupe rock streaked with layers of mauve and burgundy. The timeriders moved bravely forward until the path reached the mouth of a cave.

"Danger!" whispered Azur, her senses tingling with negative vibes.

Feeling somewhat protected within the pale blue aura that bound him to the cat, XT was the first to step tentatively through the entrance.

"I'm standing on a ledge!" he said through clenched teeth.

"Should we enter?" asked Azur.

"You don't have a choice," he said, "Step to the left and keep to the wall."

Holding their breath, Azur and Dilly stepped one by one through the cave entrance and stood beside XT on the ledge. Azur's heart was pounding so hard, she could hear its beat in her ears.

"I can't move!" said Dilly. "I'm petrified of heights."

"Stay still until our eyes adjust to the darkness," suggested XT. He hoped his voice projected a confidence he was far from feeling.

Glued to the wall in terror, they reached for each other's hands. Their ears and noses detected sulphurous fumes and gurgling, popping sounds before their vision detected that they were in a large cave containing a viscous, belching pool. The narrow ledge on which they stood encircled the pool. Two ovate portals were visible on the opposite wall of the nightmarish cave.

"I'm even more terrified of black yuk," whimpered Dilly.

"We have to make our way to those openings," said XT.

"Let's start then before we all die of fright," said Azur.

Backs pressed to the cavern wall and holding hands, the timeriders shuffled sideways towards the twin egresses. Bleu growled and hissed, electrified hues of violet, hyacinth, and ultramarine rippling through her spiked fur.

It was then the Faefumes made their first appearance. Dancing upon the malodourous pool, undulating green forms laughed and leered. "When I have fears that I may cease to be, before my pen has glean'd my teeming brain," they taunted.

"The darkness is never darkness to the One," whispered Azur, her voice trembling.

Dilly and XT added their voices to the chant. "The darkness is never darkness to the One... the darkness is never darkness to the One… the darkness is never darkness to the One… the darkness is never darkness…"

The Faefumes faded away and the timeriders, still chanting, continued shakily along the ledge until they reached the first exit. They peered through the stone portal to see a trail meandering along a winding, blue river. White, pink and fuchsia flowers lined the riverbanks.

"Okay, Bleu," said Azur. "Should we take this exit or the next one?"

The cat looked up at her with brilliant sapphire eyes. "Mrrrooow," she said without moving.

"I think it's your call, Az," said Dillian. "Just get us off this ledge."

"You haven't time for guessing games," said a voice behind them. "One of these doors leads to nowhere and you don't know which one it is. I can take you directly to Hilma and save you a lot of anguish."

The trio turned and saw Vek standing serenely on the ledge on the far side of the cave portals.

"No thanks," said Azur. "We plan to leave here tonight."

"Unfortunately your sister won't be accompanying you," said Vek.

Pointedly ignoring the Faefume, Azur made a decision. "First door it is," she said to her friends.

Single file they followed her through the opening. The trail ran alongside a serene blue-green river. On the other side, flower-bedecked meadows stretched to a blue horizon. Making up for time lost, the timeriders set off at a brisk pace.

"There's something wrong with this setting," said XT.

"What do you mean?" asked Azur.

"The scenery looks unreal."

"Doesn't everything look unreal?" asked Azur.

"They're murals!" exclaimed Dilly.

To test the startling revelation, the timeriders reached out their hands and touched rock walls on either side of the trail.

"When I behold, upon the night's starr'd face, huge cloudy symbols of a high romance," whispered a voice in Dilly's ear.

Dilly let out a yelp of fright.

"What?" asked XT and Azur, turning in alarm.

"And feel that I may never live to trace their shadows, with the magic hand of chance," sang several voices aloud.

"Keep walking," said XT, resuming the chant taught them by Zhiab. Azur and Dilly added their voices. "The darkness is never darkness to the One… the darkness is never darkness…"

Suddenly the trio bumped into a solid rock face. The trail which had appeared to wind before them was merely another image etched upon the rocky walls of Vapourlea.

Thirty-four

Initially stymied, the timeriders soon realized that the trail had not ended but merely turned abruptly to the left before leading to a lair carved into the rock. Inside, Faefumes jeered and pale timeriders from hapless journeys past lay about languorously.

"Come in, come in!" cried a Faefume holding out his arms invitingly.

Trying to ignore him, Azur turned to a pale young man leaning against the entrance. "Have you seen my sister, Hilma?" she asked him.

He replied with a negative shake of his head and gazed at the travellers with expressionless eyes.

The timeriders rushed along, turning this way and that as they searched for Hilma. Each time they encountered a lair, the timeriders warded off grasping green hands to check inside. Then, panting from exertion and fear, they raced back to the previous turn. Along the trail, green forms, whispering, moaning and jeering, bobbed and swayed.

"I'm disoriented and claustrophobic," said Azur, sinking to the floor of the forest maze.

"It will only get worse, *much* worse," said Vek, squatting down in front of her. "Stop punishing yourself and come with me."

"You need to focus," said Dilly, pushing past the Faefume to shake her friend's arm.

"On what?" said Azur in near-despair.

"On finding Hilma," said XT, sitting down beside her.

Dilly sat down too and the three timeriders, cross-legged and holding hands, formed a circle on the stone path. Bleu, her deep blue fur on end and sapphire eyes glowing, growled and hissed in the circle's centre.

Strengthened by her friends' presence, Azur closed her eyes and breathed deeply. "Chant," she told them.

Softly and fervently, Dillian and Xavier Tennyson intoned the words, "The darkness is never darkness to the One... the darkness is never darkness..."

"See you later," laughed Vek as he took his leave.

The timeriders helped each other to their feet, retraced their steps, turned left, right, left, and halted when their senses alerted them to the nearness of the sulphur pool.

"Wrong direction," said XT. "We have to turn back in order to complete this maze."

Fretting over the wasting of precious time, they turned back, made several turns and checked out more lairs until they reached a final dead end. Convinced that they had not missed Hilma, they reversed their way along the trail, exited the river maze onto the lip of the fearsome sulphurous cave. From there, they inched along the ledge to the second portal.

Within the portal, the travellers found another trail, this one entering a peaceful forest where grand oaks and graceful pines reached skyward. Again the setting was an illusion. Willowy tree branches were but patterns traced on rocky walls. Lush ferns carpeting the forest floor were mere graffiti. The timeriders picked up their pace, reassuring themselves that they could handle another painted labyrinth.

As in the previous maze, they turned left and right on paths that sometimes circled back on themselves and at other times came to abrupt dead ends. Although they continued to chant, the Faefumes buzzed about them like annoying flies. The timeriders investigated every lair they encountered but found no trace of Hilma.

At one lair, Azur glared at a Faefume who sidled up to her flirtatiously. *Don't touch me!* she messaged him silently.

Xavier Tennyson and Dillian heard her searing thought and reinforced it with their own mental commands. *Don't touch us! Don't touch us!*

The Faefume flew backwards into the lair and landed with a thump against the back wall.

Well done, said Azur triumphantly to her friends.

"You're using your mind well," said Dilly. "What about your other senses? What about your nose and ears?"

"I'm trying!" said Azur petulantly.

"It was Zhiab who told you to turn on all your senses," XT reminded her. "Are you doing that?"

"What do you think I'm doing?" snapped Azur.

"We're conceding that you have powers superior to ours," said Dilly, an edge to her voice.

"Take it as a compliment, Azur," said XT.

"I'm sorry, guys," said Azur contritely. "You're absolutely right. Enough *trying*. From now on, this is for real!"

Emboldened, and with senses ablaze, she pushed onward, pausing briefly whenever a path branched off from the main trail to sniff the air and listen keenly. Suddenly, she turned confidently down a path that seemed no different from the others. Dilly, XT and Bleu trekked quickly behind her.

When the forest maze exited into the mouth of a tunnel, the timeriders hesitated only briefly before entering the darkness. Shrieks and moans echoed eerily from the blackness that stretched before them. Bleu hissed and growled, sending sparks flying in all directions.

"The darkness is never darkness to the One… the darkness is never darkness to the One…" they chanted, illuminating their way with the light of their auras.

As they plodded through the tunnel, green speckles floated towards them like snow in the headlights of a moving vehicle.

"And when I feel, fair creature of an hour!" whispered a voice near Dillian's face.

"That I shall never look upon thee more," sang another.

"Go away!" screamed Dilly, covering her ears with her hands.

"Never have relish in the faery power of unreflecting love!" cackled a green form, rising before her.

Azur hugged her friend's trembling body. "I'm sorry, Dil," she said. "I became over-confident and stopped chanting." She and XT resumed chanting until Dillian regained her composure and was able to join in.

The chant encircled the timeriders like a comforting blanket, relaxing their tense muscles and soothing their distressed minds. *The darkness is never darkness with the One…the darkness is never darkness with the One…the darkness…*The gentle, persistent rhythm enabled them to enter the core of their beings and meld into one another's soul consciousness.

United in cosmic energy, their auras glowed with released sensointuitive powers in a rainbow of brilliant colours. Bleu's vibrant fur sparkled and sparked. *We are ready*, they communicated to each other from their hearts. Led by Azur who walked with the assurance of one whose inner compass is drawn to a powerful magnet, they hurried through the tunnel.

I'm coming, Hilma.

I'm waiting for you, Azur.

The tunnel was in fact a third maze, complete with twists, turns and lairs. This time, however, Azur's heightened senses led them directly to the lair of Vek. Hilma's listless face gazed at them as they rushed to her side, cocooned in their rainbow emanations.

"We're here to take you home," said Azur.

Hilma looked at her sister with puzzlement. "You have to stay with me," she said. "I cannot leave Vek.

"Stay with us… stay with us," intoned a small group of pale human mutants.

"Stay with us… stay with us," sang a trio of Faefumes, crowding close to the travellers.

Vek tried to penetrate the rainbow aura to ensnare Azur, Dilly and XT, and although the Faefume leader was unsuccessful, he cackled viciously. "Didn't I tell you!" he shrieked. "The girl is not leaving."

"Hilma, we've come all this way for you. We can take you safely out of Vapourlea," said Dilly.

"Vapourlea is my home now," sighed Hilma.

"Why would you want to stay here?" cried Azur in disbelief.

"I can't leave Vek," said Hilma.

"She needs me," said Vek with a smirk.

"She's intoxicated by your poisonous fumes," said XT angrily. "Look what you've done to her!"

"Hilma," said Dilly. "It's Vek that needs *you*. Don't you see? He's a vampire and he's draining you of your soul!"

Azur reached out to take Hilma's hand and was surprised to find that contact with her sister was repelled by an invisible shield.

Vek roared with laughter. "You're not the only one protected by an aura," he sneered.

It was then Azur saw the thin layer of Vek's mustard-coloured aura surrounding Hilma's lifeless white one. "No!" she screamed in frustration.

"Hilma," said Dillian gently, "remember how much you enjoyed playing piano duets with Mavis while Bram accompanied you on violin?"

"Beautiful music…" said Hilma dreamily.

"There's no music in Vapourlea," said Azur.

"No music…" agreed Hilma sadly.

"Bram and Mavis have not played music since you left," said Azur, tears running down her face. "They love you so much and they miss you terribly."

"They love me…miss me…" echoed Hilma.

"Do you love them? Do you miss them?" asked Azur.

"Yes," whispered Hilma. "I love them…"

"Do you want to see them?"

"Want to see them…" she whimpered, tears in her eyes.

At Hilma's words of longing, a small hole opened in the mustard aura surrounding her. Azur reached through and drew her sister towards her. While Vek howled in outrage, the timeriders pulled Hilma into their rainbow aura where she collapsed in their arms.

"You're out of time, you're out of time," hooted Vek.

"Run," said XT, picking up the girl's listless body and throwing her over his shoulder.

Secure in their energized rainbow, the timeriders began to run. While Vek and other Faefumes floated around them, screaming and harassing, they began to backtrack their way to safety.

The timeriders chanted steadily as they raced through the tunnel, picking up speed as they went. In a colourful blur of cosmic energy, they sped through the forest maze and into the river maze. However, when pungent fumes reminded them that they were approaching the cave with the sulphur pool and the narrow ledge, fear nibbled at their powers.

The vivid colours faded from their magnificent aura. Their feet slowed, muscles burned, and breathing came in ragged gasps. They became acutely aware of their racing pulses and the pounding of their hearts within their chests. XT wilted under the weight of Hilma upon his shoulder. Faefumes who had accompanied them as they raced through the mazes began to jeer and heckle.

It was in that moment of near despair that Azur received a vision. She saw the serene countenance of Zhiab, the smiling faces of Sean and Violet Galvinston, the procession of McConnels and Tennysons around Fletcher House, the hands of her grandmother lovingly sewing clothing for the journey. She heard the voices of children and adults chanting. *The darkness is never darkness to the One…We're with you, we're with you.*

In a burst of power she transmitted the vision to Dilly and XT. Colour flooded back to the rainbow aura, Azur's indigo prominent in the brilliant display. Bleu purred loudly, shooting out sparklers from her multi-hued fur.

Chanting steadily, they sped through the entrance of the sulphurous cave and swept across the treacherous ledge. They raced up the ramp and rejoiced to find the Vapour Gate open in the stone foundation of Fletcher House.

As their feet pounded up the cellar stairs, the sound of the bells of Steam Engine 330 preparing to pull away from Prosper Station clanged tauntingly in their ears.

DAY 11

All Saints Day

Thirty-five

Swathed in moonlight, the empty streets of Prosper Station scarcely needed the muted spheres cast by the street lamps upon the roads and walkways. Throughout the sleeping town, residences and businesses were in darkness with the exception of dim lights visible behind the drawn curtains of a few hotels.

Across from Fletcher House, the GTR station master had already bolted the doors of the wooden structure, extinguished the lamps on the lower floor, and gone upstairs to prepare for bed. The last of the workers on the loading platform were now leaving the railway yard.

The timeriders burst from the hotel's summer kitchen and raced along the path separating the rear of Fletcher House from its livery and stables. Horses, bedded down for the night, nickered and whinnied softly as they rushed past.

Their boots pounded across the boardwalk, but before they could touch upon the road separating hotel and railway, a green figure with black shaggy hair and piercing dark eyes stepped from the shadows.

"Hilma, my love," he said gently, "you know you're my favourite. Come back with me and I will give you everything you want."

Draped across Xavier Tennyson's shoulder, Hilma struggled to get down.

"Ignore him, Hilma," said Azur, reaching out to touch her sister.

Flailing about, Hilma managed to slip from XT's grasp. Before she tumbled to the boardwalk, the arms of Azur, Dilly and XT propped her up.

"Come to me," said Vek. "I need you!"

"But you don't need *him*," said XT to the girl.

"Let go of me," whimpered Hilma, pushing at the hands that hurried her along.

Half-dragging, half-pushing the resisting girl, the timeriders reached the rail yard. They raced across the tracks in front of Steam Engine 330 which, primed for departure, snorted and rumbled. The iron monster impatiently emitted noisy blasts of steam at the approaching passengers. Bleu, fur wildly on end, snarled and hissed back at the beast as she scurried over the tracks alongside XT's feet.

On the boarding side of the train, the timeriders sped along the wooden platform. Vek, keeping pace with them, was attended by several green figures who reached out with wavy, snake-like arms.

"Come back to me, Hilma," called Vek. "Come back to Vapourlea."

"You know you don't want to leave us," sang the green figures in quavery, sing song voices.

"Let go of me!" cried Hilma, clawing and kicking at her rescuers. "Let me go!"

Undaunted, Azur, Dillian and Xavier Tennyson pushed ahead, scattering squealing green forms as they ran.

Vek reached out to steal back his human prize but could not penetrate the rainbow aura surrounding the timeriders. He shrieked in outrage.

At last, the timeriders reached the lowered steps of the coach car where a conductor, smartly attired in his uniform of polished brass and navy, stood on the platform waiting to assist them.

"You're just in time," he said, reaching out to touch Hilma gently.

He turned to the rescuers. "I've already put your baggage on board," he told them.

They looked up to see the friendly face of James McConnel smiling at them from under his shiny conductor's hat.

A second conductor stood in the doorway of the coach. "You almost didn't make it," he said. "In fact, I'm surprised you did."

"We had help," said Azur, propelling Hilma up the stairs with the help of Dilly and XT. The girl's feet barely touched the steps and her head lolled to the side like a rag doll.

"You're the conductor from the train that brought me here," said Dilly in an effort to distract the man from watching Hilma.

"That I am," he said. "In fact, I accompanied all of you from Providence Crossing to Prosper Station.

"Were you expecting to accompany us back?" asked XT.

"Not really," he admitted. "You can thank your conductor friend, James McConnel, for insisting I not raise the boarding steps before the stroke of midnight."

"You would have done that?" asked Dilly indignantly.

"I always do. It gives me time to settle my passengers in."

"What if the passengers haven't arrived yet?" asked Dilly.

The conductor shrugged.

"Would you know where our baggage is?" XT asked him.

"Right over there on some empty seats," said the conductor, pointing into the coach car. "McConnel retrieved it from the station and handed it up to me as soon as the train pulled in. Told me he was counting on me being professional – as if I'd be otherwise." He chuckled ironically.

Azur looked back to express her gratitude to her great-great grandfather, but he was no longer there. *I'll be able to tell Mavis about you*, she thought.

"Let me go…let me go," mumbled Hilma feebly.

"The little one seems a tad reluctant to go home," said the conductor nodding his head in Hilma's direction.

"Not at all!" said XT.

"She likes to be independent and do everything herself," explained Azur.

"But, as you can see," added XT quickly, "she's extremely weak and needs assistance getting on board."

"I want to go back," whimpered Hilma.

"Don't worry," said Dilly brightly. "You *are* going back, Hilma, and your grandparents can't wait to see you!"

Hilda writhed and kicked. Her rescuers held her firmly, all the while keeping neutral expressions on their faces.

Outside the train, Faefumes gathered in increasing numbers. Ranting and raving, they crowded onto the railway platform and spilled over into the rail yard.

At the bottom of the boarding steps, Vek clung to the railing, spewing rage. "She belongs to me," he screamed.

"She never did and she never will, you demon monster!" shouted Azur.

The conductor looked perplexed. "Are you travelling of your own free will?" he asked Hilma.

In reply, the young woman moaned and collapsed to the floor. XT picked her up in his arms and carried her through to the coach.

The conductor hesitated for a moment before pulling up the steps. "Sorry, my friends," he said to the Faefumes as he closed the coach door. "You didn't win this time."

Howls and shrieks from the Faefume horde rose in the night air.

Thirty-six

Inside the coach car, XT carried Hilma to a window seat where she sank limply into the soft leather, her head falling against the lacy backcloth. Even in the dim illumination of the coach's oil lamps, the green pallor of the girl's skin was apparent. Azur sat down beside her, holding her thin, cold hand.

XT and Bleu sat behind the sisters and Dillian took a seat across the aisle.

"Look out your window!" said Dilly.

Azur looked past Hilma's head and saw Zhiab gazing back with his dark almond-shaped eyes. He nodded solemnly when she smiled and waved at him.

"He's so beautiful in the moonlight with his long black hair and blue skin," she said to Dilly.

"He's beautiful in any light," agreed her friend.

"Too bad I'm not a blue mutant," muttered XT from his seat behind Azur.

At that moment, the train lurched forward. The timeriders exchanged excited glances as it rolled away from Prosper Station. Once outside the town, the iron beast gave a wailing farewell whistle as it picked up speed.

Hilma stirred restlessly, uttering moans and whimpers.

"Are you okay?" Azur asked her.

"He didn't want me to go with Vek to Vapourlea you know," mumbled Hilma, her eyes still closed.

"Who?"

"Zhiab. He told me to lay low in Prosper Station until the train came back, but then Vek came along and said if I went with him, I would be a princess in his beautiful domain."

"Vek deceived you," said Dilly.

"I was happy," said Hilma, a faraway smile on her face.

"You were in a trance," said Azur.

"You were a prisoner," added Dilly.

"Why do you keep sniffing me?" asked Hilma.

"I'm not sniffing you," replied Azur. *You're exhaling fumes plus the stench of Vapourlea on you is so powerful, there's no need for sniffing*, she thought.

"Do I smell like Vek?" asked Hilma.

"Yes," admitted Azur reluctantly. *And it's disgusting.*

"I'm not ever going to wash it off," sighed Hilma dreamily.

Until Mavis gets her hands on you.

"I'll lock myself in my room," muttered Hilma.

Oh, oh. Have to block my thoughts!

The train picked up speed, its engine vibrations and the clack of wheels upon steel rails blending into a rhythmic refrain. Peering through the windows into the outside darkness, the timeriders saw their faces reflecting back at them. As on the previous trip, the train soon entered a tunnel carved into rock. It went ever faster until the stone walls blurred, and the train seemed to leave the tracks. Pushed back into their seats, the passengers instinctively grasped the leather coach arms until they could again feel tracks beneath them.

"Tickets, please," said the conductor, standing in the aisle.

They dug in their pockets and handed them over.

"The young miss doesn't have one?" asked the conductor frowning.

"How could she?" asked Azur in alarm.

"It seems that Vek didn't give it to us," said Dilly sarcastically.

Azur shot her a warning glance. *This is no time for your humour, Dil.*

"Just kidding," said Dilly quickly.

"Guess she'll have to disembark," said the conductor.

"What!" they exclaimed in unison.

"Just kidding," said the conductor. "James McConnel gave me a ticket for her."

The timeriders exhaled in relief.

"I'll be right back with refreshments," said the conductor.

He wheeled a cart up the aisle and set portable tables before each seat. With a flourish, he covered each table with a linen cloth and placed serviettes upon his passengers' laps. On each table he set plates of fancy sandwiches and cakes.

"Tea, Mademoiselle?" he asked Azur.

"Yes, please," she replied, "and some for my sister."

Soon Azur, Dillian and Xavier Tennyson were sipping tea from gold-rimmed china cups adorned with the railway logo. Hungrily, they munched the dainty sandwiches and cakes. Hilma, however, showed no interest in food or beverage.

"Have some tea," said Azur, holding a cup to Hilma's lips.

The girl took a sip and began to choke. "I don't want any more," she said.

"A bite of sandwich? They're delicious."

"No." Hilma closed her eyes and moaned softly. Her skin glistened with perspiration.

Azur wiped her sister's face with a serviette.

When the timeriders finished eating and drinking, the conductor placed the linens and empty dishes on the cart and wheeled it to the back of the car.

"Get ready," said Dilly. "This is when we all nod off."

"I hope I can stay awake and keep my eye on Hilma," said Azur anxiously. "I should have resisted the refreshments."

"Let's keep talking," suggested XT. "That should help us stay awake."

"Pick a topic," said Azur, too stressed for creative thinking.

"We can talk about what we're going to do after we get home," said Dilly.

"That would be interesting," said XT. "What will you be doing, Dilly?"

"I'm going to finish my year in fine arts. Then, in late May, Graeme Kilgour and I will marry."

"And after that?"

"Graeme plans to attend teacher's college next fall. He wants to teach high school. I'm getting into digital graphics."

"Do you think you'll return to Providence Crossing?"

"We'd certainly like to. It's our dream to raise a family there, and I'd like to have an art studio in the town someday."

"And you, Azur?" asked XT.

"I need a couple of courses and a bunch of intern hours to complete my program," she said, knowing that they already knew this.

"And when you're finished?"

"I'll come home to help Bram and Mavis with Hilma. That is, if they don't want me to stay home now."

"You mustn't lose any more study time, Azur," said XT. "I'll help your grandparents manage Hilma's rehab."

"It's the day to day care that could drain Mavis."

"I don't think you need to worry," said XT. "Your grandmother will whip up some of her specialty brews and all will be well."

At least until next Hallowmas, thought Azur grimly. Aloud she asked, "What about you, XT? Are you going to stay in Providence Crossing long?"

"Of course! I have a practice. And I have a lot of research to do."

"And when you complete your research?"

"It depends…"

Azur felt a twinge of anxiety which was quickly replaced by an awareness that the neurologist was silently laughing in the seat behind her.

As the timeriders vainly tried to fight off drowsiness, Bleu jumped down from her seat beside XT, stepped over Azur's feet and leapt on the seat between the sisters.

"Mrrooow," said the cat to Azur, looking up with expressive sapphire eyes. Then she snuggled down next to Hilma and laid her head upon the girl's lap.

"Thank you, Bleu," said Azur. "Keep her in her seat until we arrive."

The cat growled reassuringly.

Within minutes, Dilly and XT were soundly sleeping and, despite her efforts to resist, so was Azur.

At her slumbering sister's side, Hilma lethargically stroked the deep blue fur of the family cat.

"I don't think I need rehab, Bleu," she murmured. "Do you?"

All Souls Day

Thirty-seven

"Pros-per!" announced the conductor.

The passengers stirred themselves awake as the train braked to a stop, clanging engine bells announcing its arrival. The conductor handed down the baggage to a waiting porter who set the luggage on the loading platform.

Xavier Tennyson took Hilma's arm and guided her to the coach car door. From there, he and the conductor helped the girl down the stairs. Azur, Dilly and Bleu followed.

The platform they stood on was dimly lit by a single gas lamp. The dark outline of the wooden station was eerily visible in the moonlight.

"We're still in Prosper Station!" gasped Dilly.

The timeriders looked about in shock and horror. A smile crossed Hilma's face.

Then, in a flash, the scene changed. The train, conductor and porter disappeared as did the gas lamp and the wooden station. The timeriders baggage no longer lay on a wooden platform, but on the cement and tarmac parking lot of Providence Crossing Public Library. Overhead was the roof of an area which, on Saturdays, housed the Farmers' Market.

"It's too bright!" complained Hilma, shielding her eyes from the electric lights that hung from above.

The small group of people who had been waiting anxiously at the back of the brick and stone library rushed towards them laughing and crying.

Bram and Mavis Galvinston hugged and kissed their granddaughters.

"We were so afraid you wouldn't return," said Bram tearfully.

"Vek... Vek.." whimpered Hilma.

"What are you saying, sweetheart?" asked Bram.

"She's delirious and needs to be nursed back to health," said Azur.

Dilly was amazed to be greeted by her mother and fiancé who embraced her warmly. "What are you doing here?" she asked them.

"That's a fine welcome," said Graeme Kilgour. "Did you think we wouldn't find out about your escapade?"

"Mavis told me where you were, dear," said Edith Witherton, "and although I was skeptical, I felt obliged to inform Graeme."

"I was beyond skeptical," said Graeme.

"And now? asked Dilly.

"Give me time," said Graeme cautiously.

Dilly wrapped her arms around him.

"You really frightened me, Dil," he said. "I thought I might never see you again."

Xavier Tennyson thoughtfully watched the family reunions from the sidelines. Seeing him standing there alone, Dillian brought Graeme over to meet him.

"You were on this mad adventure too, I see," said Graeme after Dilly completed introductions.

"I was," said XT.

"So you're one of the senso..."

"Sensointuitives," completed XT. "No. I'm just an ordinary guy."

"How did you come to be with them?" asked Graeme.

"It's a long story. You and I will have to get together sometime when you're in town and do some sharing."

"I'd like that," said Graeme. "Right now I'm feeling bewildered and… hurt that I wasn't included.

"Azur needed me," said Dilly. "I didn't want you worrying or angry."

Graeme shrugged, indicating that he was both.

Noticing that the Galvinstons seemed to be struggling with Hilma, XT walked over to stand beside Azur.

"Vek…I want Vek," whimpered Hilma.

Mavis threw a questioning glance at Azur and read the answer in the older girl's eyes.

"You don't need Vek anymore," she told her younger granddaughter.

"Let go of me," said Hilma, pushing roughly at her grandfather's hands.

Bram studied his granddaughter sadly. The bright, healthy girl he remembered had been replaced by an irritable young person who reeked of fumes and whose clammy skin was a ghastly colour he had never seen before. "You're unsteady on your feet and seem unwell," he said evenly. "I believe you can use some help."

"Well, I don't," she said sullenly.

"The moon is in the ideal phase for banishing addictions, illness and negativity," said Mavis mildly.

"But just for a few more days," muttered Hilma.

"That will be long enough for a good start," said Mavis.

Hilma snorted.

"I'll be around to help whenever you need me," said XT to the Galvinstons.

"I appreciate that," said Bram. "It would seem we'll definitely be requiring some professional consultation."

Hilma glared at them all. "Is today All Souls Day?" she asked.

"Yes," said Mavis. "Why do you ask?"

"The real Samhain has already passed which means the door to Vapourlea closed two days ago." She sniffed morosely, rubbing her eyes against her sleeve.

"All Souls Day celebrates souls who have been rescued," said Bram, opening the car door and ushering his granddaughter into the back seat. "It's the perfect day to welcome you home."

Bram loaded XT's and Azur's bags into the trunk while Mavis went around the car to sit beside Hilma.

"Are you my bodyguard?" asked Hilma.

"No, darling. I'm your grandmother."

"…who's always been there for you, I might add," said Bram, climbing into the driver's seat. As he did so, Bleu slipped through the door and jumped across to the front passenger seat.

Hilma scrunched her eyes tightly shut, pressed her hands over her ears and hummed tunelessly.

"Hop in the front, XT, and I'll drop you off at your place," said Bram through his opened window. "Azur can squeeze into the back."

"Thanks, Mr. Galvinston," said XT. "If it's okay with Azur, I'll walk her home before I go back to my apartment. We mightn't have a chance to talk again for a while."

Azur gave her grandfather a self-conscious smile. Wordlessly, Bram shut his door and the Galvinstons drove away. Dillian, her mother and fiancé followed in the same direction in Graeme's Toyota Corolla.

Side by side, Azur and XT left the downtown streets and walked at a leisurely pace towards the gothic homes of Crescent Park. Their boots and Azur's long skirt swished through leaves fallen from the mostly-bare trees. A mild breeze, warm for early November, caused branches to gently sway.

Azur jumped when something dangling from a tree brushed her cheek.

"It's only a scarecrow," said XT, pulling her close.

Azur snuggled against him, inhaling his comforting scent. *Am I as appealing to you in the real world as I was in Prosper Station?* she wondered.

"You've bewitched me since the first day I met you," said XT.

Startled, Azur looked up at his face. *Are we still thought sharing?*

"Guess it hasn't worn off yet," he said, smiling. "And, if we're kindred souls, as Violet called us, perhaps it never will."

Are we fated to fall in love? wondered Azur. She tried to quiet her thoughts, wishing she were doing a better job of keeping them to herself. *I'll need to practice thought blocking.*

"I'm already in love with you, Azur," he said seriously, "and I hope you're fated to fall in love with me."

"Stop reading my thoughts!" she exclaimed. "I like to mull things over and not go rushing headlong."

"I'm not in any hurry," he said, removing his arm from around her.

Immediately she regretted her words. "Don't move away," she said, reaching out to touch him. "We've known each other barely two weeks and I really, really like you. Maybe I love you." *Certainly, you make me ache with longing.*

"I like cautious people," he said, mollified.

They had reached the stairs leading to the entrance of her house. The verandah light was on, and XT's back pack lay on the top step.

"I wonder if that's a signal that I'm to go no further," said Xavier Tennyson.

"Let's go around to the side," suggested Azur.

He looked at her searchingly. Then laughing, they walked hand-in-hand to the ungated side of the house where sheltered in the thickness of a cedar hedge, they exchanged a long, passionate kiss of promise.

ABOUT THE AUTHOR

Gloria Pearson-Vasey is a storyteller who weaves magical realism and contemporary issues into her works of literary and science fiction, mystery and historical fantasy.

A member of The Writers' Union of Canada and Crime Writers of Canada, Pearson-Vasey's background includes nursing, psychology, music, journalism and theology. Inspired by her autistic son's unique sensory experiences, her writing reflects the hidden nature of things.

She lives in a picturesque Ontario town, enjoying nature, country drives, reading, and time with family.

Visit Gloria's website http://www.gloriapearsonvasey.com to read more about her books.